Mike & Bec

by
Tom Vazzana

DORRANCE
PUBLISHING CO
EST. 1920
PITTSBURGH, PENNSYLVANIA 15238

This is a work of fiction. Names, characters, places, and incidents are either the product of the author's imagination or are used fictitiously, and any resemblance to actual persons, living or dead; events; or locales is entirely coincidental.

Dorrance Publishing Co
585 Alpha Drive
Pittsburgh, PA 15238
Visit our website at *www.dorrancebookstore.com*

ISBN: 978-1-6376-4337-2
ESIBN: 978-1-6376-4649-6

Mike & Bec

"Fiction can hit close to home."

The author wishes to thank his family, friends, and colleagues. You all are part of *Mike & Bec*.

Special thanks to the security guard in the White House bathroom.

CHAPTER 1

I sat in the corner of the dimly lit room, knees to chest with my arms wrapped around them. I could see Mike lying on the bed about 10 feet away. The room was unremarkable, except that it was a hospice room. That's a room for a patient to be made comfortable as their time on Earth begins its end. While the room was regular, it was Mike who was remarkable.

I knew by the repetition and regularity of the machines beeping, and by Mike's breathing, that this would all be over in less than 24 hours. Mike would leave this world, and I, Mike's Soul, would rejoin the Others. I may be placed in a new person or may be left to spend time with the Others and recharge.

I had been through this before. Many times. More than many...thousands of times since there were people. I was neither ready to move on or stay. This was not my choice anyway. I did want a bit more time with Mike, but this was our time together in the way of the order of things in the After Place.

There are some people who I liked to remember after it was all said and done. And there were some people I did not like. It's okay not to like people on Earth. In the After Place, all that kind of stuff is forgotten and, while not forbidden, is just unnecessary. On Earth, it's really a matter of personal taste.

I liked Mike. We had many adventures and so many personal encounters with other fantastic people that I had never experienced before in my countless eons in the After Place.

Some of my other favorite people were:

Diane Poltawick, 1933. A wonderfully eccentric nut job...but high-functioning in a crisis.

John Clemmons, 1635. Stable as a rock, full of trust, he was respected by all and loved a good laugh.

1950s, Danny Zimmer. A Broadway baby who was in every show ever. Mike would have liked him quite a bit.

Then there was Mike's gang, who just played games until the wee hours of the morning. Andy, Donna, Brian, Patty, the other Patty, and Janine. This gang was always fun and up for a caper. They would spend hours planning heists that would never happen. They also had a lot of laughs. Laughs that would bring you to the point of almost vomiting. I liked to think they brought a lot of laughter to others, too. All of them have passed now...except Mike.

Being in Mike as his Soul brought a lot of firsts. In previous people, I had never lived a lifetime in an Italian household. The loudness and vibrancy of that life were fun, disturbing, disruptive, public, loving, and crazy...with an emphasis on *crazy*.

I had never jumped off a cliff in South America and parasailed. Oddly enough, neither had Mike. Mike convinced these Brazilians running the ramshackle "parasail cliff experience" that he, indeed, was a certified parasailer. No one asked for documentation; they just asked Mike if he was certified. And without hesitation, Mike said, "Yes!"

Sounded more *certifiable* to me.

Before Mike, I had never whitewater rafted for over a hundred miles in Bali. I had never worn a mink stole, sung a cabaret song, and threw back a Gimlet...at least not in that order.

So, leaving the Earth again and leaving Mike behind, I decided this time I should just sweetly and slowly drift off. I did not want to bolt out of the room when it was done, as I did with other people like William Stuckard. I had a terrible Soul-life experience with that especially stupid man, but you'll hear about him in a bit.

A Soul has some power over the final moments. Not too much control, but they can fight to linger a bit longer or just decide to lift and go. William

Stuckard was a definite lift and go. Known as William, Bill, Billy, or Will, Willy Stuckard was so stupid that I bolted out of that room as soon as I heard him exhale his last breath.

Why do I think Stuckard was so stupid? There were so many reasons. He was not the smartest person in the world, and that's okay. It's just that he had so many opinions about everything that made no practical sense. He would start almost every sentence with, "Well now, that can't be right... " and then he'd go on about politics, the economy, if you are tending the lawn correctly, if you're tying your tie wrong, if it was too cold or hot, that everyone at work was wrong about something... It went on longer than this paragraph.

So why did I choose to spend time with William Stuckard? I must have previously been in a person who was so smart, it was irritating. Maybe I was in Einstein, or Benjamin Franklin, or Ruth Bader Ginsberg. Well, it wouldn't be Ruth. She and Mike were alive at the same time. But someone like her. Maybe Harriet Tubman; someone great like that. Maybe I needed a break.

So, I bolted when Stuckard checked out. Like punch-out time on *The Flintstones*. Yeah, I watched *The Flintstones* because Mike watched *The Flintstones*. Wilma and Betty just killed us both. "Charge it!" If you don't get the reference, it doesn't matter. This is Mike's life, not really yours. If you don't get something...just wait...something will end up resonating with you. And this is the story of Mike and I, so we can get off William Stuckard for now.

I wanted to drift out, lightly leaving Mike because I loved Mike, and I liked Mike. Mike was fun. Mike is fun...he's just not the life of the party right now in the year 2050. Mike is currently at Pullman's Hospice in a small town in Maine on the craggy shores of a quiet beach. This was where Mike wanted to be in his last hours.

After Mike passes, he and I will never meet again. That's how it works. Mike will be united with loved ones of the past. I know you have all been waiting to hear about that. Yes, you do get reunited with everyone from your past. But with that, you also meet everyone who has ever lived and passed. That's a lot of people. Luckily, there is an eternity, and there's always someone new to meet every second. It can be daunting, and it can be fun. Oh, and if you happen to get introduced to William Stuckard—run.

When Mike finally passes, he will feel slightly empty, tranquil, and lucid, but look transparent. Mike will get used to this new sense of being and begin a life as a part of a larger thing in the After Place. I just don't know what that "larger thing" is.

Sitting in the corner, now with my legs more relaxed and my arms loosely hanging by my side, I began to remember...

CHAPTER 2

Before I was Mike's Soul and so many others' souls, I was Bec. I am Bec. My name has no known origin to me. One of the Others must have chosen it. Or it was always my name. It's not really a name, but more of a feeling...no, a sound...a sound that resonates like *Bec*.

Bec is hard to describe, but let me try. You know the sound a moderately priced crystal wine glass makes when you twang it with your fingernail? Not a Target wine glass or a high-end Tiffany's wine glass...more like a HomeGoods wine glass. That twang is Bec.

The name Bec suited me, so I liked it. Bec sounds, in your language anyway, like it may mean strong and mystical. I am one of those things. I'm not strong. Souls are not strong, as they do not need or acquire physical or mental strength. We are more consistent than strong, and I am, by nature, the quintessential mystic. While there is no sense of explanation of a Soul, there is purpose to a Soul. A Soul is, always has been, and always will be. I know that concept is so difficult for people to grasp; that a thing has always been around. But it is true. There's no real answer that started it all. It's just faith that makes the whole thing work.

You see, we Souls do not control our person. We are along for the ride. We don't impact a person's decisions. We are the engine in the car. The Soul keeps the life energy going, but the steering is done by the person. A person cannot live without the Soul, but a Soul can be without a person for a moment, for a lifetime, or for an eternity.

The Soul does take part in the nonverbal part of the conversation or selection process of the next person to receive a soul. They hear about the new person before they are born and what that person's journey will most likely be. The Soul then decides to join in the person's life or take a pass. It all depends on what the Soul has yet to experience.

You should know that a Soul forgets all that initial decision-making once they join with the person. Once they become one, the Soul loses all memory of past experiences, only becoming conscious again of itself and the person—Mike, in this instance—in their last hours. And that is when the Soul separates to begin the reflection of their journey together.

I was the Soul of many different people from all over the world. Talk about the quintessential learning experience... Before I joined Mike in 1961, I was the soul for Helen Gander Dunbar.

I particularly liked Helen Gander Dunbar, born May 14, 1902, in Chicago, Illinois. She was brilliant. Not at birth. She became brilliant a bit later on in life. As a child, she drooled and pooped, just like everyone else, but her mind grew to be as sharp as a tack. She would turn out to be a genius, although Helen did suffer as a child from malnutrition and melancholy. Her parents were Francis and Edith. Francis was an electrical engineer, and Edith was a professional genealogist.

It was when little Helen was misdiagnosed with polio that her interest in the science of medicine began. By the age of 12, she had a theory that physiological medicine was conjoined with psychosomatic medicine. She believed that both were needed to repair a person's health.

And not to diminish Mike, but at 12 years old, Mike was still performing the alphabet on Gramma Cecilia's kitchen table.

Helen was a force to be reckoned with, standing four feet, 11 inches. She always wore platform shoes; not like ABBA, but more practical and demurer—and absolutely no glitter.

Helen was also a very heavy drinker.

In our last moments together, I asked, "Helen, why did you drink so much?"

Helen wheezed and said, "Because I was an alcoholic."

Mike was not an alcoholic; he is dying of old age. I have separated from Mike, and now, we begin the process of reflection.

So, let's go back to the start. It was an easy decision for me to become Mike's Soul as I really liked the description of his life to come. And, for the record, I loved every minute of our time spent together for his entire life. Let's talk about the concept of time for a moment. Time is a definite "thing" on Earth. During his life on Earth, Mike and I experienced the same time-line. And once Mike passes and I drift, we will both remember all that time. Now, time does not just disappear, and no, you do not enter a timeless par-adise. Trust me, there's time. There's just so much time, there is actually an Other whose job it is to track all that time. Sounds like an awful job.

The expression, "You have too much time on your hands," is a good thing in the After Place. Odd how that is perceived as a bad thing on Earth. Really, all you have on your hands is time. Mike will not know he had a physical life and a separate Soul who moves on until the very end, at his last few seconds of life. Again, it's just the way of the After Place. And once there, Mike will just be Mike, "sans Bec," if you will. Slightly a bit more ethereal, like on a good solid dose of Xanax.

I wasn't born or trained or selected or once a person. I just am, always have been and always will be. This is my, how shall I say it...? Well, it's my job. There's no 401K. How I exist is beyond my capability to understand, and I don't really need to know because I never will know. I'm not even going to theorize about it. All I know is that I am not an Angel; they are something else altogether. Though I don't know how Angels become An-gels, I know they are sent from the Source, and Angels do influence your life and decisions.

Angels are sent with a specific purpose. You've heard about some fa-mous Angels, many of whom have been captured in the gorgeous paintings of the Renaissance Masters and also can be seen in the not-so-gorgeous paintings of the Dutch. Angels wait around being all Angel-like until they are called upon for their critical message they must bring to a person. It is considered an exceptionally honorable role.

Angels tend to be uppity at parties in the After Place.

Mary's Angel—you know, the famous one?—announced Mary's preg-nancy to her using a loud trumpet and booming voice. Maybe a nice note passed to her would have been a better choice, you know, not to alarm, scare, and awaken the entire household. I mean, it was the middle of the night. Mary certainly had some explaining to do in the morning. Here's how it may have played out.

MARY

Good morning. Perhaps you heard last night the windows break and an Angel yell, rather loudly, that I am with child.

MARY'S MOM

Oh, that's nice, Mary. Will you pass the goat's milk and honey?

MARY'S POP

Mary, is that Angel gonna pay for that window?

I don't think it happened this way, but what do I know? I am only a Soul.

Let me be clear: Mary was informed by an Angel that she would give birth to a child of great importance. However, the Angel did not give further details, like that the child would grow to be a man who gathered a flock of worshippers, talked about a better life with God, carried a huge cross and the burdens of the world on his shoulders, and then died on the same cross he had to carry.

That was all Mary's child's decision. The Angel was just the catalyst, and all of that is just what happened. All the decisions and preaching and living a life of service was by Jesus' choice. This is an amazing example of the triumph of what a person can do in their lifetime.

Chapter 3

Mike seems stable right now, lying in bed. The beeps sound the same. I am still sitting in the corner. I've watched people come and go as they check on Mike. There are no visitors. It wasn't that Mike didn't have any friends or family. Not at all. In fact, it's quite the opposite. It's just that Mike was single and had lived so long that he had outlived his family and many of his friends. Honestly, Mike looked bored but pleasant.

Bored and pleasant can basically describe Mike in general. Mike could literally have everything in the world around him, and he would like it for a minute, and then he'd be bored. He once got a birthday card from a friend named Jodi with a picture of a little boy sitting in the middle of hundreds of toys and a book called *The Everything in the World Book*. There was a thought bubble above the little boy's head on the card, and that bubble had the text: "I'm bored." It was the perfect card for Mike. Mind you, this is not to be confused with Mike being boring. Mike Pennello was definitely not boring.

I don't know if Mike can recall his life during these last hours, but I hope so. There is so much to revel in and remember.

Chapter 4

M̲ike Pennello was born on May 19, 1961. The number one song on the radio that day was "Runaway" by Del Shannon.

"Never on Sunday" was the song that won the Academy Award that year.

These two tidbits of information don't matter. Mike didn't particularly like either of these songs, although he could belt out "Runaway" loudly in the garage, basement, or living room. I only mention it now because Mike loved music and movies so much. Mike would always equate an event to a song or a movie or a Broadway show. Those were his timekeepers—the songs, the movies, the Broadway shows... What outfit Cher was wearing...

Who needed a Rolex when you had Cher's outfit to tell you what decade you are in historically ?

Let me tell you about Mike's birth.

Mike finally popped out of his mother, Maria, like a pent-up cork in a bottle of sparkling wine. It took a while, the labor, but then...*KABLATT!* The doctor did not even have time to say, "Now, one last push." Mike jumped outta there and quite literally was never going back in.

The nurse asked what the baby's name would be. Maria, Mike's mom, immediately blurted out, "David." So, they wrote down David Gerard Pennello on the birth certificate. David's father, Sal, had no idea where the name David came from. The story goes that Sal went home that night, couldn't sleep a wink, and could not stand the thought of his son being named David.

Sal came back to the hospital the next day and said, "Maria! Why David!?"

Maria said, "I don't know. It just felt right. I didn't give it too much thought. I just had a baby. I liked the name."

"But, we will not... I will not have a child NOT named after me!"

"Sal, I would rather die than have this child named Salvatore. Where do you think we are, in a small town in Sicily?"

"Oh, I didn't know you hated my name," said Sal.

"I don't hate your name. I mean, I don't love it, but I love you, and I call you Sal. This baby will be David. And that is done."

"David Pennello? That sounds like an Italian Jew..."

Maria said, "I think that's a beautiful mix." Maria liked it, but Sal continued, "This baby will not be David."

Maria said, "It will be David."

This went on for quite some time until a nurse came in and said, "Is there an argument going on here? It's a bit loud from the nurses' station."

Sal says, "Nurse, Maria named our son David."

"Yes, I know. I wrote it on the birth certificate."

"I hate it."

"The birth certificate?"

"No, the name."

"Well, it has been about a day, and the paperwork is done, so his name is legally David."

Maria piped in.

"See, Sal...David. Nurse, Sal wants to name David the crazy name Salvatore."

The nurse made a very distorted frown.

"Oh, no. God, no. That is an awful name for 1961...or ever. Unless it's the name of a nice Italian restaurant, then it's okay."

Maria said, "That's what I said! Plus, it is legally David now."

Sal said, "Is there any way around this?"

The nurse asked, "Do you even have another name picked out?"

"Linda," Maria said. "Linda was the other name. You see, my mother-in-law, Cecilia, hung a gold chain over my belly when I was eight months pregnant, and it swung in a counterclockwise circle, and Cecilia said that was a sign it was a girl."

A bit confused by this new medical phenomenon, the nurse said, "So, you would like to rename David to the name Linda?"

Sal said, "No! Of course not."

"It was just the other name that I chose, Sal! The nurse just asked what the other name I chose was, and it was Linda."

The nurse said, "Well, I think we can all agree that Sal is a bad name."

Sal said, "Well, I don't agree..."

Maria said, "Sal. Shut up. Nobody cares what you think."

The nurse continued, "Sal, what is your middle name?"

"Michael."

The nurse smiled.

"Well, that's a lovely name. Maria, do you like Michael?"

"Yes. I do!"

"Well, I'll be right back, and we need to keep this a secret." The nurse returned with the birth certificate and a pen.

"Now, I'm going to cross out David, here, and replace it with Michael. I'll just tell everyone I miswrote the name, and it'll all be fine. No one will be the wiser." Maria and Sal thanked the nurse. Now the nurse leaned in and said to them in a hushed tone, "Now remember, let's keep this between us, you know...about 'David.' Keep it low. No one should say...'David.' I'm going to take the fall for this, and everyone will be happy. Whatever you do, just nobody say 'David' again."

They nodded in agreement.

And at that precise moment, Maria's hospital room door swung open and Rose, Maria's mother, basically screaming, says, "Oh, where's my little David? That David. I have six balloons that all say, David. See? David... David...David... David...David...David!"

Rose was followed by Cecilia, Sal's mother, carrying a big wreath of red and white carnations in the shape of a horseshoe that read, *God Bless David*.

Maria got a bit nervous.

"Ma...Ma...Ma..." Then to Cecelia. "Ma...Ma...Ma..."

Sal said, "Everybody, shut the hell up!"

The hospital room went silent. There was a pause as Rose and Cecilia looked to both Maria and Sal.

"Did David die?" asked Rose.

Cecilia asked, "What has happened to David? Oh, I knew I didn't say enough rosaries last night!" Cecilia dramatically looked up to the heavens. "Why did you have to take David so young? And before being baptized! Now he's going to have to be in purgatory with all the Chinese babies."

Maria said, "Ma...no... David is alive...his name, not so much."

Sal said, "We changed it. I could not leave my legacy behind being named 'David.'"

Rose said, "Oh, my gawd. Oh, my gawd, no. You did not name that baby Salvatore, did you? Cecilia, he's your son, and even you would agree that David shouldn't be named Salvatore! Where the hell are we, Sicily?"

Sal shrugged to himself and said, "I don't think it's that bad a name."

Cecilia said, "Sal, it's a dumb name, and Rose and I agree. I didn't have a choice. I had to name him after his grandfather Salvatore on my side of the family in the Italian tradition. If it were today, I would have named him Anthony."

Now Rose and Cecilia bantered back and forth like they were having coffee at Woolworth's.

"Oh, that would have been nice, Cecilia...Anthony. What a nice ring to that."

"I know, Rose; isn't Anthony a nice name?"

"Cecilia, Anthony would have been a good name. Yes, Anthony. I like that."

"Yeah, and you could call him Tony or Anton. There are so many possibilities."

Maria said, "Can we get back on the subject? Our son's new name is Michael."

The room was silent for a moment. Then Rose said, "I love it!" like she was remarking about a new hat.

Cecilia said, "Yes...and that's your middle name, Anthony...I mean Sal."

Frank and Jim, the grandfathers, popped all the balloons that had the name David on them and took the ribbon off the red and white carnation horseshoe, and so that's how Michael was "David" for a day.

Now, let's go to the day before—the day of his birth. Mike was born with a full head of hair, and Rose said to Maria, "You see, Maria. I told you that's why you had so much heartburn. All that hair. Right, Cecilia? I told you about the heartburn. That's why you had heartburn." Rose leaned in really close to Maria and said extra loud and slow, like Maria spoke some other foreign language. "Maria, the hair on the baby's head gave you the heartburn. All those months of heartburn were because the baby was born with a full head of hair...like Liberace hair. That's why you had so much heartburn. I told you about the heartburn, Maria."

Mike's grandfather Jim said, "That is the ugliest baby I have ever seen," and took a puff of his cigar...in the room. It was allowed then. Unbelievable.

Aunt Connie piped in with, "Maria, look; you had a boy! Look at that beautiful boy. Too bad you had the girl first, but now you have a boy! Thank God. A girl is nice, but a boy...well, it's a boy, and that's just better than a girl."

How many friggin' people were in that hospital room at Saint Mary's on the Hill? Also, for the record, there was no hill. But the hospital was named Saint Mary's on the Hill. Anyway, Maria was barely conscious. She had been given the twilight drug and could barely feel a thing. However, Maria could hear everything and never wished to hear the word "heartburn" ever again.

Meanwhile, Mike's dad, Sal, was in the hall. He didn't feel well. They should have given him the twilight. Maria and Sal loved Mike, and they all came home three days later. That's when Mike met his sister, Gloria. She seemed nice, I thought. Mike wouldn't know. Mike was barely awake at 72 hours old. Gloria was already four and had many opinions about everything. She did not yet have an opinion about Mike though. She had more opinions about her goldfish, The Supremes. Yes, I know this name implies more than one fish, but oddly enough, this one little goldfish was named The Supremes.

Gloria was the one with the talent for sports and took after Sal, but she was way prettier. Gloria ended up excelling at almost all sports. It's like she intuitively knew how to just pick up a racket, play tennis, throw a football, be the best shortstop, bowl, kick a soccer ball, and even play lacrosse.

Mikey played baseball once in his life and was put in right field—the best spot for the worst player. Someone hit a ball to right field, Mikey caught the ball, which shocked everyone, but he broke his entire hand, ulna, and radius. He had caught the ball with his hand without the baseball glove. Mikey was unclear on sports rules.

Mikey liked musicals...even *Damn Yankees*, and that was about baseball. But they were dancing baseball players, so that made it okay. He lived in a suburb of New York City. I remember that Mike's first memory was the sun rays streaming through the window of his bedroom, but that's hazy at best, so let's jump forward five years.

That birthday was a milestone. Five! Wee! The number one song on the radio was "The Battle of the Green Berets." Again, this information is as unimportant as it was unfortunate. Why was that song popular? Can you sing it? Are you still alive to remember it?

In the year Mikey was five, the 1966 Academy Award went to the film *A Man for All Seasons*, and the number one song was "Summer in the City" by The Lovin' Spoonful. *A Man for All Seasons* was a bit beyond a five-year-old's comprehension, but Mikey did love "Summer in the City." It had the words "hot down" in it. It sounded fun, and Mike would say "hot down" as much as he could before he eventually got slapped by someone. Now that I am thinking about it, I'm pretty sure the lyric was "hot town." He was a funny kid, that Mike.

Mike received a really fantastic plastic boat from Cigar Grandpa Jim on his fifth birthday. Mike loved that boat more than anything ever. It was his favorite toy. Becoming five years old also meant the first day of kindergarten at Saint Blaise, the patron saint of tending to a choking boy. Is it just me, or is that just oddly specific for a saint's only role? I mean, shouldn't a saint have more than just one job? Would Blaise be a bit more useful if he were the patron saint of both boys and girls who were choking, or everyone who was choking, or even people with mild coughs? This just seemed like a bit of a waste of sainthood.

The Others and the people in the After Place don't choose saints. Living people pick the saints. Keep that in mind. People elect a number of questionable politicians. Keep that in mind also. On the first day of kindergarten, Carrie Tinito poured green paint down Mike's brand-new velvet-like shirt during art class. Mike loved that shirt. His mom bought it at the JC Penney at Culver Ridge Plaza. Mike was so excited to wear that shirt on his first day of school, and he was so mad after the paint incident. That day, Mike learned that kindergarten was overrated, and so was Carrie Tinito. That was day one at Saint Blaise's.

That was also the day Mike learned about revenge. Was it a coincidence that Carrie Tinito had a very interesting and nearly impossible accident in the cloakroom where she interestingly and unexpectedly fell onto her prized marching band baton and lost her virginity at a very early age? Now, don't let me mislead you. Mike was nowhere to be found, and Mike did not use force on little Carrie Tinito. Mike had a shirt dripping with paint from that little freak of a child, and he went into the cloakroom to take off the wet shirt with paint on it and put on a smock that Mrs. Reeners, the teacher, gave Mike. While in the cloakroom, Mike saw that awful Carrie Tinito's spangled baton lying flat on the floor below Carrie's coat.

Let's stop for a moment. Why was it called a cloakroom? Was it the late 1700s, and we were all vampires with cloaks to shield us from the sun? We had coats. Call it a coatroom. My God!

Okay…so, Mike did enter the cloakroom, and he did move that baton… and the cloakroom wasn't lit up like a bowling alley, making it hard to see, so he might have stood the baton upright between Carrie Tinito's boots, and it may have been a trip hazard, and that could have been how little Carrie Tinito popped her cherry. We all believed that doctors were able to reattach everything. No one ever really checked or asked, frankly.

Carrie Tinito ended up as Carrie Flannigan, the wife of the man who invented the Mood Ring and other heat-sensitive materials for a large photographic company. They had a mansion on the lake, destroying the myth that you needed to be a virgin to marry well in 1980.

The only lesson I can figure out here is to definitely learn to twirl the baton.

CHAPTER 5

I am one of billions. There is a Soul for each person who is on Earth. Even when there were only a few thousand people on Earth, the tally of Souls in the After Place was exactly the same as if the Earth was at its peak population. If all the Souls stood shoulder to shoulder on Earth, they would fill the Shetland Islands' size, including the Isle of Man. Surprising, right? You thought it would be bigger. Me too, but some Other tallies that, and so, there you have it. You just have to trust it, because it is true.

This fact makes me think about people. There are roughly 8 billion people on Earth. What country would be the size needed if all 8 billion stood shoulder to shoulder? And the answer is... The state of Maine. Again, surprising. You thought it would be bigger. I know, and I agree.

And why are both of these places with Souls and people standing shoulder to shoulder, rugged, craggy, coldish, meandering road landscaped, coastal places? You'd think Texas or Saudi Arabia. Nope...Maine and the Shetland Islands, inclusive of the Isle of Man.

Enough of that.

I don't call myself Bec for me. I call myself Bec for you because that's the closest to that sound on the wine glass...remember?

A Soul is the link to the Source. This is where you think it will get complicated. It's not. Each person's Soul has a line to the Source. There are so many lines to the Source that it all looks like one line. When Sondheim said in his groundbreaking, albeit exceptionally long musical *Into the Woods*, "No one is alone," he was right. If people could just see this vast array of

Souls for themselves, they would never feel alone. Their line to the Source is hugely intertwined and conjoined to so many other people.

And yet, Mike felt lonely many times during his rather adventurous life. And not just Mike. So many others. So many.

Mike knew he was never ever going to be really happy. Mike knew he would have moments of happiness, but he always knew he would never feel happy. I never really understood why the Source would not make Mike happy. Maybe Mike was created to make others happy.

Oh! The Source. Okay, I don't know what that is.

We are told about it in non-word sounds, and we just accept it's a thing, and we know it's a good thing, and we, as Souls, don't get to see the Source. I know you thought for a moment that I would be able to explain the great mystery of life. I can't. I cannot explain the grand mystery of life because this is the way the Source likes it. Is the Source selfish or selfless with this mystery? I don't know.

The Source is like the Stanley Kubrick of the After Place. Leave them guessing about what the hell is going on for hours, make the plot painfully slow and monotonous, and have a weird ending. This pretty much sums up life.

CHAPTER 6

Mike, Mikey to some, was 10 years old in the year 1971. The number one song on the radio was "Joy to the World" by Three Dog Night. This is kind of important. Mike found his voice in this song. He loved to sing this song at the top of his lungs. Mike was a singer.

Mike lived in an old firehouse restored by Cigar Smokin' Grandpa Jim into a multi-unit complex housing his aunts, uncles, both sets of grandparents, cousins, and an awkward family no one really knew because they were just renters. They were the Abkows.

There was a store on the ground floor, and everyone had to work in the store. Except for the Abkows...the renters. Stock the shelves; wash the floors; snap, break, and cut the chicken's head off; de-feather it; wash it; bind its legs; and then place the decapitated and bound chicken in the refrigerated showcase. You know, normal stuff. It was like a commune, but with more yelling, clean clothes, and red meat.

Saturday was fishing day with Cigar Grandpa Jim. All the kids went: Mikey, Gloria, Johnny, Augie.

Johnny and Augie belonged to Aunt Connie and Uncle Del with the boy obsession (Connie gave birth to two boys). Uncle Del's name is really Delmonico, named after Grandpa Jim's father, as Italian tradition dictates.

Cigar Grandpa's name was, as I said, James. Jim. His birth certificate called him Vincenzo. But his friends called him Lenny, and the family called him Zeke. Grandpa Jim was married to Cecelia, named after the patron saint of singing. Finally, a saint that makes at least a modicum of sense.

Cecilia was the ruling matriarch of the family, and no one did anything without Cecilia giving the okay...along with Rose, of course. Rose was the other matriarch in the firehouse apartment complex. Rose was Maria's mother. Cecilia and Rose ran that apartment building. They consulted each other on all matters, and Rose and Cecilia would cut your throat open to save the family—or if you cheated at Pochinno, an Italian adaptation of Bingo... As if anyone needed an adaptation of Bingo.

The men did not matter, except for show, like show dogs. In public, oh yes, your husband is an equal partner. But at home, you would hear, "Get the hell out of our way, boys, and give us the checkbooks to balance because you are idiots."

Maria was the only child of Rose and Frank. Cecilia and Jim had twins named Delmonico (Del) and Salvatore (Sal). Rose, Frank, Jim, and Cecilia lived in two units behind the storefront on the first floor. Del married the irritable and lovable woman named Cicungetta. Everyone called her Connie. Aunt Connie.

Aunt Connie was like a cow who gave silky and yummy milk but then kicked over the pail just in spite, so you could not drink any. I think in Italian that translates better. Del and Connie had the two boys, Augie and Johnny. They lived on the third floor.

Grandpa Jim had three sisters. Angelina, Jenny, and Nancy. Angelina played the honky-tonk piano at the Beer Garden Saloon and at the silent movies back in the silent movie era. Angelina was a hoot, and she loved a good party. She was fun, and the room always lit up when Angelina walked in.

Jenny, her older sister, stank of whiskey and always wore a sweater even if it was 95 degrees. And a sweater clip. If you don't know what a sweater clip is, then you're either young or not Italian. An Italian woman wears a sweater draped over her shoulders, but the arms are never in the sleeves. So, to keep the sweater from slipping off, you used a sweater clip. Two sprung pinchers at the end of a short chain. One side would pin to the left side of the sweater and the other to the right, holding the sweater in place, not falling off your shoulders. Add this to the long list of things I learned from Mike.

Nancy, the eldest of the three gals, was always whistling; the first sign of crazy, according to Mike. They lived on the second floor. None of those gals married, and no one ever wondered why.

Maria, Sal, Gloria, and Mike lived on the fourth floor. There was no elevator. Maria had fabulous legs after hauling babies and groceries up all those flights all those days. The Abkows lived on the fifth floor, and we never saw them. There is not much to say about the Abkows. There was some history here of how they knew Grampa Jim, and it had something to do with the cold storage of furs.

Yes, that's it. There was a place the Abkows owned called The Fur Studio, where people stored their furs for the summer months. This was an actual thing, and people obviously had enough furs to need them to be stored. I think Grampa Jim bowled with Mr. Abkow, and they were friends and became renters. They were very silent and kept to themselves. This was a good choice.

Who would want to join all the levels of crazy below them? The Abkows had two very pale children named Christopher and Gisella. Oh, they were German. Mrs. Abkow would sometimes yell out the window, looking for Christopher, "Chris-ti-fah!" Just like that. Chris-ti-fah. Why couldn't she just say Christopher? I mean, she had no trouble saying Gisella. It's practically the same sound. They end the same. What was up with the Chris-ti-fah?

One day, Mike ran into Christopher in the stairwell and asked him why his mom always called him Chris-ti-fah. He gave a surprising answer, and one Mike did not expect.

"She's not my mom," he replied, and he ran up the stairs. Well, that just became a fantastic mystery.

Mike told his mom, and she told him to not get involved and it was none of his business. In Mike's mind, they were a German spy family unit. Mike shared his theory with Gloria.

"Oh sure, Mikey. These German spies decided to live above an Italian insane asylum to learn all our secret pasta recipes to share with all the hidden Nazis hiding out in the United States and send the best pasta recipe back to Germany."

Gloria had a bit of an attitude. Years later, Mike found out Gloria and Gisella were actually really good friends.

They just didn't want to get the whole family involved in the friendship. And Mike's family always got involved with the friends. If you were a friend, you were family, and you had to work in the store and, more possibly, get slapped by Aunt Connie.

CHAPTER 7

Mike was a singer. He could sing the alphabet standing on top of the table in Gramma Cecilia's kitchen. He was 35 years old, but that didn't matter to him. That kitchen table was his stage from five years old to 10 years old.

He was no Pavarotti, but Mike wasn't Yoko Ono either. Mike liked to sing, and he discovered he liked to act out plays in the backyard. He put on lavish one-man shows that nobody watched, and he produced and directed some shows with the neighborhood kids. Most notably was the revival of *Alice in Wonderland*.

Mike wanted to play Alice, but Gloria's blue dress did not fit him. And that is the only reason Mike did not play Alice. Mike played both Tweedles in a remarkably bad costume made up of two pairs of Grandpa Jim's fishing pants. Mike was in his world and thriving in the make-believe. Maria and Sal knew it. They were worried, not so much that Mike wanted to play Alice, but that they thought he would actually have been a better Alice than Gloria.

Gloria was stilted in the role. Everyone said the show should have been called *Tweedles in Wonderland*. Mike agreed, but the entire family apartment complex taught him never to brag. You could gloat, but not brag. Gloating was quieter and harder to detect by neighbors.

Mike became the star of mostly all the shows in grammar school at Our Mother of Perpetual and Everlasting Sorrows. (Sidenote: How sad could she possibly be?) Mike played in *Our Town, You Can't Take It with You,* and the unlikely hit, *Hedda Gabler*. This is how Mike learned to be a woman scorned. He didn't play the title role of Hedda Gabler, of course. That role went to Susan Ashton with the port-wine stain on her neck. She, at least, had a reason to be scorned. Mike had perfect skin and was scorned that he didn't get to play Hedda.

He gloated about his skin for all four hours of *Hedda Gabler*. The kids all thought they got a standing ovation at the end of *Hedda Gabler*. They did. All the parents had to get blood back into their asses from sitting those four long hours. They shot up like rockets. Some had trouble getting up because their legs went numb. Ibsen could write so well, you became lame.

When Mrs. Sampleton, the English teacher and drama club moderator, announced the children would premier Victor Hugo's *Les Misérables* next semester, Cecilia and Rose threatened to cut her throat. Needless to say, there was no Les Miz. After *Hedda Gabler*, Mike leaned more into musicals. They were peppy and had more costumes.

In eighth grade, Mike wanted to put on a production of *Grease*. *Grease* was still running on Broadway, so that was out of the question. So, Mike wrote his own version of *Grease* called *Soda Shoppe Boys and a Few Girls*. Somehow, Mike convinced Principal Sister Stephania—a handsome woman who looked like a linebacker or a roller derby gal—to use the school's theater club money to fund this show.

Mike's show had the same premise as *Grease*, but the guys had all the lines and songs, and the girls always seemed to be carrying large boxes. The music was all from the radio of the 1950s, and Mike choreographed and directed the whole show. Now the school really had something to be perpetually and eternally sorry about.

Mike graduated from Mother of Perpetual and Eternal Sorrows in 1973 and went on to high school at Christ the King of All Mankind. See, Mary didn't need to be all that perpetually and eternally sorrowful, but it worked out well for her son, and he got a school with a really hard name to live up to.

CHAPTER 8

Now I am standing at the foot of Mike's bed. I find myself humming "Rock Around the Clock" from *Soda Shoppe Boys and a Few Girls*. Mike is resting, and the machines still making the same noises. Things are progressing, though. I can feel the cord between us getting just a tad tauter as the process of being pulled back to the Others happens. It's a beautiful thing, really; knowing you are part of something greater. Knowing that Mike is part of millions of people waiting for him.

It's not the same for me. This is Mike's moment, and I am the camera that captured all the moments of Mike's life. I am the reflection of Mike. I know that when Mike finally decides to leave, I will drift to the Others. There won't be a discussion of, "What was your person like? Was it fun?" This is not how it works. I know I have to enjoy Mike now because I, as a Soul, may jump into another person again almost immediately and forget Mike until that new life is done.

The film *Ice Castles* popped up in my reflections of Mike's life. *Ice Castles*. Boy, Mike liked that film. We watched that film at The Waring Theater about seven times. The year was 1978. Colleen Dewhurst was amazing. Mike liked her gruff kindness. Every time, near the end of the film, the girl's skating was building to its gorgeous climax, and the crowd in the ice rink stands began to throw stems of beautiful roses onto the ice. Mike would yell out, "She can't see the roses. She can't see the roses. She's a blind skater!"

Mike thought he could fix it for Lynn-Holly Johnson. But he couldn't. She would fall, literally blindly, skating onto the roses, faltering and falling, showing everyone that she was a blind figure skater and was still brave enough to compete in the Midwest Eastern South Figure Skating Finals. Mike always teared up for Lynn-Holly Johnson. Mike was that kind of guy.

A nurse enters the room, and I find myself interrupted out of lightly humming the song "Through the Eyes of Love." The nurse checks Mike's vitals, and then he leaves the room. Everything is on track, and then I feel the gentle tug of the cord again. Yes, all is on track.

I like these moments best. Maybe 12 hours until the end. Twelve hours to enjoy the reminiscing of life with Mike. With Mike? About Mike? About me? I guess it all applies, and with that, I float to the ceiling to look upon Mike from a new angle. And that's when I remember something. *The Poseidon Adventure!*

Chapter 9

In the 1972 hit movie *The Poseidon Adventure*, Shelley Winters played a long-distance swimming medalist. She, well, her character, helped save all the people trying to escape the good ship *Poseidon*. You know, the capsized luxury cruise ship that was a movie blockbuster?

Mike watched that movie so many times, and he loved so much about it. He loved Shelley. He loved the Christmas tree climb. He loved Carol Lynley lip-syncing to Maureen McGovern's voice, and of course, he loved the misguided people who he thought were so stupid, going up to the top of ship—which was upside down—so that meant they were going deeper into the water and then they died...mostly from stupidity. In his many discussions about the film, he would say, "Why didn't they listen to Gene Hackman? He had an Oscar, for God's sake!" That always bothered Mike.

Mike began high school in 1975 at Christ the King of All Mankind. You should have heard the school pep rally cheer. It literally took four minutes. Try spelling out rhythmically "Christ the King of All Mankind." It was exhausting. It was not as easy as yelling out "Wheel...of...Fortune!"

During his freshman year, Mike learned how to play the trombone—badly. He was in the play *High Hopes*, then *Jesus Christ Superstar*. He went to class, too. Mike was popular because he was funny and in all the shows. It was like being in all the sports, but with more costume changes.

Mike had the best joke of the year in his freshman year...at Father Debler's expense. There was a huge mass on the stage of the auditorium. The entire freshman class was there—every one of them. Christ the King of All

Mankind was a huge school with 500 students in each class. That makes 2,000 shining Catholic boys and girls, folks! The school was one big building cut into two identical halves: One side girls; one side boys. Seniors could cross over and have mixed classes...so progressive.

Anyway, Father Debler was getting all into his Mass, explaining the different parts to the children, just as the sacramental hosts arrived at the stage.

Bringing the hosts to the altar during mass was a big deal. I mean, you were chosen for that. At this particular Mass, the chosen ones were Andrew Cala and Steve Calzone.

Father Debler became very dramatic. He said this was a "miracle" they were all going to witness when the bread on this altar would become the actual body of Christ. Father Debler shot both his arms up into the air and said, "I am now going to perform..." and Mike yelled out from his seat, "A cartwheel."

Well, there was no recovery for anyone after that. The choir director, Sister Mary Joseph (there were like 18 Sister Mary Josephs and an equal number of Sister Joseph Marys), laughed so hard that snot shot out of her nose. And, as the kids in the seats squealed with delight, Sister Mary Agnes's (the typing teacher) face cracked the only smile she ever had in her whole life. And Susan Ashton...you know, Hedda Gabler...laughed and farted loudly. It was an amazing moment in time!

Mike thought the school should have been renamed Mike the King of all Mankind.

CHAPTER 10

At school, Mike and his best friend, Andy, wrote an insane musical called *Getting Ready*. It took five years to write, but it really only had an opening number.

> *Getting ready isn't easy*
> *When you're running a half hour late.*
> *Getting ready isn't easy*
> *When you have a punctual date.*
> *The clock ticks down.*
> *The bells will chime.*
> *Why, oh why, do I never have...*
>
> [four-beat pause]
>
> *...enough time.*

Okay...not even an opening number. More of an opening verse, really. But they saw potential there. I mean, Mike said he sat through *Passion* on Broadway and thought their song's lyrics were better—way better.

One day, Mike found Andy running down the stairs from the abbey; the top floor of the school, not like *The Sound of Music* abbey. It was just the upstairs where the Brothers and Sisters who taught at Christ the King of All Mankind lived and probably drank heavily.

Andy ran right into Mike and breathily began his loud whispering: "Oh my God! Brother O'Connor just asked me if I would consider becoming an Irish Christian Brother!"

"What?"

"Oh, my God, Brother. O'Connor just asked me if I would consider…"

"No, I heard you; I just meant, what?!"

"Oh…Well, Brother O'Connor asked if I…"

"Oh, my God, I heard that part!"

"Oh. Well he asked me if I would consider becoming an Irish Christian Brother!"

"What did you say?"

"I said YES…but only because Brother O'Connor is so handsome. I got thrown by his good looks and his Stetson cologne. I just said, 'Yes!' Now, I'm worried I'm going to have to be a celibate Irish Christian Brother."

"Andy, you're not capable of being celibate even though you're still a virgin."

"Debatable…and I know."

"Well, wait. Do you want to be a Brother?"

"I mean, except for wearing the black gown and the really cool rosary bead belt, no, not really."

"Just tell Brother O'Connor thanks for the offer, but you've changed your mind."

"I can't. I'll clench up. I won't be able to do. The Stetson cologne, Mike. The Stetson is my kryptonite. Will you do it for me?

"Me?"

"Yes. You're the one that knows the right thing to say at the right time."

"May I remind you of the 'cartwheel' incident at mass?"

"Yeah, right. Oh! I'll have my mom send a note. Or wait. I'll have my doctor say that it would be unhealthy for me to be celibate because of some biological issue. No. Maybe my mom should call and say that I have deeply soul searched, and I just don't feel the Brotherhood is the best choice for me. Then she could say I've become despondent, worrying that I would disappoint every known Irish Christian Brother.

"Andy, you're over complicating this. You are being so *you* right now. You're making this so dramatic. You make everything so dramatic. "

"That's the meanest thing you have ever said to me. This incident will not be easily forgotten."

And with that, Andy turned on his heels and trounced back up the cement stairs, muttering, "You think you know someone...well, this is never to be forgotten."

Mike knew Andy wouldn't even remember they had the conversation when he woke up the next morning. Mike, however, would torture himself feeling that he hurt his best friend. That's how Mike was.

Mike was also a bit jealous. Why hadn't Brother O'Connor asked if he were interested in becoming an Irish Christian Brother? Why was Mike left out? Wasn't he good enough? Wasn't he at least good enough as Andy? Was Stetson really that good a cologne? Why had Mike always preferred Aramis?

It was a long night.

Mike that night thought, *I really don't want to be a Brother. I just wanted to be asked.*

Thank God a musical, incidentally a musical about God, helped Mike forget he was not asked to be a Brother. Mike had now been asked to be a devoted follower of Jesus in an over produced high school musical production of *Godspell*.

Yes, Mike was cast in the spring musical *Godspell*, and it was during this show when Mike decided to make a career out of being an actor.

People laughed at all his lines. People cheered for his songs. It was this show where Mike learned how to manipulate an audience with a line reading or a joke. Being in *Godspell* was like being in Heaven to Mike.

Mike did a terrible actor thing in *Godspell*, and well...in almost every show he ever did. There's a part at the end of the show where the guy who plays Jesus says, "One of you will betray me." The cast of playful and loving clowns each, one right after the other, earnestly will say, "Could it be me, Lord?" Well, Mike was fifth to say the line, "Could it be me, Lord?"

Lori went first. "Could it be me, Lord?"

Then Joe. "Could it be me, Lord?"

Then Pam.

Then Donna.

And then...a long pause. It was Mike's turn. Mike decided he would pretend to be busily tidying up after the last supper scene (as any self-respecting Italian would), and the whole cast was looking at him, awaiting his line. The audience was waiting. Mike looked up and waited for just the *perfect* timing and said, "Well it wasn't me. I think it was him," and pointed to the kid playing the Judas role.

I'm sure Mike would like to think that the auditorium of Christ the King of All Mankind still echoes with the laughter from that moment.

CHAPTER 11

It was 1979, and Mike was enrolled on scholarship into Manhattan College in the Bronx. Yeah, weird...I know, but when Manhattan College was built, it was part of the Island of Manhattan, then it became part of the Bronx. I don't know why. The Source may know, but the Source won't reveal the info, so there you go.

The number one song on the radio was "My Sharona." Everyone thought this new British group, The Knack, would be the new Beatles. No, bigger than the Beatles. Wow. That went all wally, now didn't it? They were one-hit wonders.

Manhattan College was an easy decision for Mike. He wanted to go to college anywhere in NYC, and Manhattan College was the first to accept him one year in advance of enrollment. Easy-peasy. Mike, Gloria, and Andy went to the school for a tour. They finished the tour in half an hour, jumped in a taxi, and went to see *A Chorus Line* at the Shubert Theater. The ticket price was $10, but that experience for Mike, Andy, and even Gloria was worth $10 million.

Mike knew that he would be a journalism major in the School of Journalism with a double major in Business and Religious Studies. He also knew he would never work in those fields. He would live and breathe theater.

Now, Grammas Rose and Cecilia said Mike needed to get that "theater thing" out of his system. Like it was a virus. Mike played along. After all, how long did they have to live? It was when the rest of the family kept saying he needed to get that theater thing out of his system that Mike became irked.

So, he did the only thing he could think of: Got an agent and starred in an Off-Broadway show at St. Marks, and then got nominated for an Obie Award in his senior year of college. He even made Manhattan College give him six credits for the show because it took so much of his time. He also graduated summa cum laude and was the valedictorian. However, Mike could not make his valedictorian speech as he had a show to do. The entire group of journalism graduates came to the show that evening. That's how you "get something out of your system."

Mic drop.

Mike really doesn't recall much from the college years. He was an ace student and missed only one day of class in four years. The day Karen Carpenter died. Mike couldn't get out of bed to get to class. Mike loved Karen Carpenter's velvet clarity, and he was devastated. He was also placed in the total jock dorm. The building was called Saint Joseph's at Manhattan College, a Jesuit College.

The rooms were fire traps, and he realized very quickly that while all the other guys were listening to hard rock, his endless playing of Donna Summer's "On the Radio" meant this dorm life would be a mismatch and not a great experience for him.

He did find his groove with the Theater Club, and that's where Mike thrived. He found his tribe, his people, his gang that loved to go to the Starlight Diner at 11:00 P.M. and have bagels with French fries and ketchup. The gang would all pile into John Kroger's car to get Ray's Pizza...downtown in the Village. The only good one. Mike was happy, but he could not wait to get out of college and begin his life. That is how Mike felt all four years.

CHAPTER 12

Wait. We need to go back to May of 1983. The hot song on the radio that year was The Police's "Every Breath You Take."

That was the year Mike graduated summa cum laude. But there was a twist to the story concerning his final dissertation for the School of Journalism. He was busy in "that play" and had to write his final dissertation over spring break. This was the quintessential piece of work that was to define a person's entire life and career. You were assigned an advisor and had monthly meetings to discuss your topic. Mike wanted his thesis topic to be totally unique—never done before. The only rules were that the topics needed to be grounded in literature, art, marketing, broadcast journalism, news, or pop culture. What's left...the work of the sommelier?

It was required that you present your final thesis to your class. You submit your thesis, which is 50 percent of the grade, and the oral presentation with visuals and the use of editing stood as the other 50 percent of your grade. Apparently, your outfit didn't matter; Mike felt that was a missed opportunity.

Day of presentation. Two presenters. Mike and Kelly Ryan.

Kelly Ryan always wore three Izod brand polo shirts over each other. That was "the thing." Bulky socks and layers of Izod shirts. It's so hard to get the Izod colors to pair nicely as it is, let alone in a triad. Here's the scene. Kelly Ryan gets up there wearing her three Izods (pink, green, and blue). It looked like a horrible flag of a horrible country that doesn't exist. Kelly had all three collars in the "up stiff" position. She looked like a very confident turtle. It gets worse. Hard to believe. But here is her thesis: "The Cigarette Industry's Marketing Strategy for Spring Breakers." Yup. Basically, Kelly Ryan went on spring break to Fort Lauderdale, smoked free cigarettes, and wrote about that.

Mike was next. He felt pretty confident, as his topic was how the 1930s German female film director Leni Reifenstahl used the machination of the human form in Hitler's commissioned propaganda film and how The Olympiad influenced the work and choreography of Busby Berkley's musicals. Kelly Ryan got an A. Mike got a C+.

What?! A C+? That stupid smoker got an A, and Mike got a C+?! That would ruin his perfect 4.0 average over four years, and he was not about to have that! So, Mike marched into the School of Journalism Dean's office. The Dean's name was Fran Broderick, and she looked exactly like Rosalind Russell in *Gypsy*. Identical. Eyebrows and all. Mike presented a well thought out argument of the resources he had to find in order to write this very specific and important thesis. He explained the time and money he had spent at the Museum of Art, Film, and Television on 6th Avenue to watch these films. There was no YouTube or Google yet. And then after he pitched what he liked to call a "big old gay screaming fit," he got that C+ turned into a B+.

It still wasn't good enough, but a win is a win, and that's why it was so hard for him to watch Rosalind Russell films after that. Except for *The Trouble with Angels*. Mike loved that film. He especially loved when Rosalind Russell hugged the coffin of her dearest nun friend who died and dropped a single tear. Rosalind Russell gave a solid B+ performance.

And who won that thesis battle? Mike, the recipient of a lame B+, for a compelling comparison and analysis of a Nazi propagandist's view of the human form thus influencing the symmetry and exacting techniques used by Busby Berkeley in *The Gold Diggers* of 1933, or Kelly Ryan who went to Fort Lauderdale and smoked free packs of Marlboros and received an A?

Yup...that's right. Kelly Ryan.

CHAPTER 13

Other than that fabulous Rosalind Russell casket moment, there was something about that 1966 movie *The Trouble with Angels* that Mike related to. The film starred Hayley Mills in the role of Mary Clancy, a young girl sent away to Saint Francis Academy Catholic Girls Boarding School and convent. Mike may have related to all of that, too.

Hayley Mills played a feisty and fun gal who always had a scathingly brilliant idea to get away with something peculiar, like sneaking down to the convent kitchen and eating ice cream after lights out, or anything to pull one over on the nuns. Every idea of Mary Clancy's went crazy-wonky, sending the nuns into a frenzy. She planned these amazing schemes with her classmates, but no matter how wonky, everything still seemed to work out well in the end. If you get a chance, you should watch this movie because it's sweet and funny and shows the transformation a person can make. No spoilers here.

In true Mary Clancy fashion, Mike had many scathingly brilliant ideas that went all kinds of crazy-wonky. One of those brilliant ideas happened with Mike's good friend, Justin B. Hayford. For whatever reason, Justin always used his middle initial, "B," as part of his name, whether written or spoken. In the film, Mary Clancy had a friend named Marvel-Ann...strange name, but although she usually bore the brunt of these ideas gone wrong, Marvel-Ann was always up for the adventure with Mary Clancy. Justin was basically Mike's very own Marvel B. Ann.

This is the story of the air conditioner.

Mike and Justin lived in a small Manhattan apartment on West 45th Street, just a stone's throw from the Milford Plaza Hotel, the Martin Beck Theater, the Imperial Theater, the Music Box Theater, the Plymouth Theater, the Royale Theater... Basically all the theaters. The district was called Hell's Kitchen. More practically, it should've been called Theater's Hell's Kitchen.

To be clear, Mike had three different apartments at 341 West 45th Street. Not all at once, but he sure was a mover! Anyway, Justin came down just for the summer to visit Mike, and they shared a 200 square-foot studio apartment. This apartment had a window, and that window opened directly to a brick wall. It was close enough to stick your arm out until you could touch the building next door.

Well, it was the middle of summer, and because of the close proximity of buildings and lack of any breeze, this studio became hotter than a Ray's pizza oven. Ray's in the Village. The good Ray's. Not the other Ray's.

Mike's parents were always there for him, and in a phone call, Mike described how hot it was and how he and Justin were barely able to get comfortable or sleep, and that it was unbearable. Mike's father, Sal, was always the first to want to jump in and fix a situation. Sal immediately called Mike back on the telephone and said he ordered an air conditioner from Gimbels Department Store, and it was going to be arriving by UPS. Mike and Justin were thrilled beyond belief that they would soon have air conditioning! This was monumental news, and the boys acted like they just won the Publishers Clearing House Sweepstakes.

Sal was always there to save the day. This is true. Mike's father worked pretty much all the time, and so there wasn't a very strong established relationship between Mike and his dad because his dad was always on the road, working. Everybody understood this and knew that Sal was doing all this work for the family. It may sound strange, but it was just accepted that Sal was not around for dinner or around the house all that much, and frankly, no one really cared. It wasn't that they didn't love him deeply; it's just that there were so many people around, it was barely noticeable that he wasn't there. This is not a slight to Sal at all. It's actually a great compliment to Sal, who was a workaholic. He was a workaholic because he cared deeply about how the family would grow and prosper and be somewhat respected and important in the community.

So, back to the air conditioner. The air conditioner arrived by UPS in a very large box. Delivered to the reception desk, Justin and Mike carried the box upstairs to their apartment. It's difficult to call that prison cell of sorts an apartment because it really was just a room with a small stove and a sink and a tiny bathroom, and, of course, that weirdo window. Justin and Mike carefully removed the packing tape on top of the UPS box and bailed out about a million pieces of peanut-shaped packing foam by the handful. Then they pulled the air conditioner out of the box with the glory in their eyes as if they'd just been handed the Holy Grail.

Justin opened the window, which wasn't an easy task because all the years of repainting the room had pretty much sealed the window shut. They finally got it open and placed the air conditioner in the window. They were stupidly excited. That is until they realized that the electrical cord to the air conditioner was not long enough to reach the electrical socket on the other side of the room. Believe it or not, this apartment only had one electrical socket. If you think about it, it makes sense because the room was so small, it only needed the one socket.

So, Justin and Mike removed the air conditioner from the window, placed it on the apartment floor, and went out to the local hardware store down the street to buy an extension cord. Once in the extension cord aisle, they saw only one extension cord left: A bright orange industrial cord measuring 500 feet long. Of course, that was too long, but they needed it, so they bought it. This was, to them, a triumphant purchase.

They hurriedly got home and put the air conditioner back in the window, closing the window to secure the air conditioner. I use the word "secure" lightly because they didn't use any support screws or even duct tape, which fixes everything, to secure the air conditioner into the window. They were on the fourth floor of this apartment building with a series of fire escapes twisting and turning past all the other studios on that side of the building, all the way down to the back-alley street level.

With the air conditioner "secured" in the window, they then plugged the 500-foot extension cord into the air conditioner, lacing the other 450 feet of it all around the room, and plugged the male end into the sole socket in the room. I think the extension cord wrapped around the room at least three times before it was actually plugged into the wall. It looked either ridiculous or like an art installation, potentially called "The Waste of Mankind."

Once they got the air conditioner in the window, Mike decided that they should make a big deal out of turning the air conditioner on. To him, it felt like it needed a ceremony. It felt like it needed a prayer. It felt like it needed an entire mass held at Saint Patrick's Cathedral. They needed to mark this moment for some reason, probably because they had a lot of time on their hands, but more probably because they were hot as hell.

I think Justin said some words like they were standing over the burial of some recently deceased pet or how the world was a better place due to the appliance's arrival. If I recall it correctly, Justin's words did feel meaningful, but in a really stupid way. Then it was the moment of truth. Mike moved over to the air conditioner and turned the dial to "COOL." The unit began to sputter at first and made an "air conditioner has gone on" sound. Then it began to blow out cool air into the studio. Justin and Mike began to jump around the studio like giddy schoolgirls at Saint Francis Academy when Mother Superior announced the theme for the annual formal prom.

The air conditioner began to shake a bit. Then it shook a bit more, most likely because it wasn't secured to the window. Then the air conditioner began to shake a lot. It rattled and shook so much that it actually lifted up the wooden frame of the window and then proceeded to fall out of the window.

Justin and Mike could only look at each other in astonishment. And as they looked at each other, the looks of horror grew as they heard the air conditioner hit each and every fire escape landing along the way down the four flights until it crashed into the alley below.

And that wasn't the worst part.

As the air conditioner fell out the window, the stupidly long extension cord began to whip around the apartment, hitting the walls, lamp, stove, and bed, all the while entangling the boys into a 450-foot orange electrical cord straight jacket. To fight themselves from being tied up, the boys spun around together to get out of the cord, looking like they were performing some wild street jump rope dance.

As a final insult, as the very end of the electrical cord pulled away from the wall socket, it delicately grazed Justin's cheek, as deftly as a kiss from Satan. Justin and Mike then watched the very end of the extension cord fly out the window, looping and whipping downward, finally lacing itself over the flattened and destroyed air conditioner. There was a moment of silence. There was a moment of disbelief. And there was wee bit of blood coming out of Justin's cheek.

Justin said something like, "Shit."

Mike added, "Holy shit!"

Then they both had the same unspoken realization. What if the air conditioner hit somebody down in the alley? They both immediately ran to the window, pushing their heads through to make sure that no one had actually been killed by the air conditioner. Luckily, no one had been down there in the alley. There was a collective sigh of relief followed by another moment of silence, then a chaser of the two of them breaking out into hysterical laughter that lasted about a half-hour. And then suddenly, Mike's laughter stopped short.

He said, "What am I going to tell my dad?" Then Mike had one of his *brilliant* Mary Clancy ideas. He told Justin that they would just say that the air conditioner arrived damaged and didn't work. That way, Mike's father would just send for another one. This seemed to make complete sense to Justin and Mike. So, Mike went to the telephone, called his dad, and said that the air conditioner was damaged upon arrival and that they needed another one. Mike thought that would pretty much solve and put an end to the situation. Mike's dad usually didn't get upset about these things and just clicked into action. He would just use his credit card to order another air conditioner, and the world would continue to spin, and the apartment would once again be cool.

Yeah. No.

Mike must have caught his dad on a weirdo day because Sal had a screaming fit over the phone. He swore at Gimbels Department Store. He screamed about UPS's incompetence, and he said that he was not going to stand for this kind of treatment and that he would take care of this. Mike pleaded with him that it was not necessary and all they needed was another air conditioner. Sal was not having any of it; he was going to make such a big thing out of this that it felt like it was going to go to the New York State Supreme Court if the matter wasn't settled to Sal's liking.

Sal told Mike he would call him back with what was going to happen next. Mike and Justin were amazed that this was not going to be as simple as their plan. They waited for Mike's dad's phone call. The phone call came about an hour later, and it went something like this.

"Mike, I've talked to Gimbels Department Store, and they blamed UPS, saying the air conditioner was perfectly fine and in working order when it left the store. I told them how upset I was about their service and that Gimbels was supposed to be the standard of great service in New York City. Then I called UPS and demanded a refund and a replacement."

Mike and Justin felt like this didn't sound too bad. Then Mike's dad kept talking.

"UPS is sending out an inspector tomorrow to look at the unit to see how it was damaged in transit. They have to fill out a full report before a refund and replacement can be processed. They're coming tomorrow around noon. Please let me know how the interview and inspection go."

Okay, that just got really bad for Mike and Justin. Mike had to come up with a scathingly brilliant idea. The first thing they did was go down to the alley below and bring the completely flattened air conditioner back up to the fourth floor. Literally, they could've used it as a coffee table. It was that flat.

Mike said to Justin something like, "Let's just put the air conditioner back in the box, put all the foam peanuts back in the box, close it up and just let them come and look at it! They'll see that it's been damaged in transit, and I think all will be fine, and we'll have a new air conditioner." So they did just that.

Feeling satisfied with their plan, Mike and Justin sat down to a bowl of cereal.

The next day around noon (UPS is very punctual), they got a call on their intercom from the front desk saying that UPS was downstairs and wished to make their inspection and file a report. Mike told the receptionist to please send them up. Mike and Justin looked at each other very self-satisfied, but then Justin's face turned pale and expressionless, looking like he had just died. Mike asked what was wrong, and Justin said in a grave monotone, "The box."

"What do you mean, 'The box'?"

"Well, if the air conditioner got so incredibly damaged in delivery, why would the box be in perfect shape with all the foam peanuts intact, yet inside the box would be a very flat, destroyed air conditioner?"

"Oh, my God!"

Mike, thinking quickly, and one might say irrationally, said, "Kick the box, NOW! We have to kick the box!"

There was a knock at the door.

The whispers between Mike and Justin went something like this.

"What are we to do now? I don't know! We should do something... We have to kick the box! But the UPS person will hear us kicking the box! I know. Wait! I got it! You cough while I kick the box. Cough? Yes! Cough loudly! It will cover the kicking of the box sound!"

There was a knock at the door again. Mike said, "Just a minute, please," as Justin started coughing like he had tuberculosis or consumption or death.

Mike began to kick the box at all corners.

They heard a woman's voice outside the door.

"Hello? Is everything alright in there? It's UPS. Hello?"

"Yes! Just a moment, please. My friend Justin is busy coughing." That sentence seemed to make sense to Mike at the time.

When Mike felt the box was sufficiently damaged and Justin just couldn't muster up another cough, they both took a deep breath and opened the door. Standing in front of them was a handsome woman, seemingly very fit, and one might say...large. Her UPS uniform was impeccable.

"Hi! I'm Mike Pennello. I am the father who bought the air conditioner...I mean, I'm the air conditioner. I mean, my father is the one who bought the air conditioner. The damaged air conditioner...the air conditioner that's damaged here in the box...from the delivery." Gesturing to

Justin awkwardly, Mike said, "This is my friend, Justin B. Hayford. He's visiting me for the summer."

Justin added a single cough.

"I'm Eunice Becker with UPS Customer Complaints. I have to review the delivery, assess the damage, and fill out a report."

Silence.

A long silence.

Quizzically looking between Mike and Justin, Eunice said, "I usually have to actually come inside to inspect the damaged goods to fill out a report."

"Oh. Yes. Come in," Mike said.

Miss Becker said to Justin, "That's a mean cough you got there."

Justin said, "Thank you."

Mike added, "Justin has this very bad cough that makes him stomp his feet."

That also made sense at the time.

Ms. Becker said, "Uh-huh."

Ms. Becker had a clipboard holding many papers and several pens in her pocket, and a pencil in her hand.

She said, "So, that's the box?"

Mike looked around the room, all 200 square feet of the sparse apartment, and then back at the box and looked up and said, "That's the box."

Justin pointed to the box and said, "That one," which was stupid because there was clearly only one box in the room.

Ms. Becker moved toward the box and began to delicately open it up and poke around as Mike and Justin slowly backed away from her in tandem. She made a lot of odd little noises inside her mouth and kept looking up at the boys. She made several notes on a piece of paper and lifted up pieces of the box using the end of her pencil. Then she lifted the flattened air conditioner, an amazing feat as that air conditioner was heavy, on its end, and looked at it very closely. Then she looked at Mike and Justin with the most judgmental face Mike had ever seen. More judgmental than any picture of Carl Gustav Jung ever captured. That's pretty judgmental; you should look that up. Then she looked at the open window.

Damn, they forgot to close the window.

Then she looked at the 500 feet of bright orange extension cord jumbled up on the floor. Then she cleared her throat.

"So, the appliance arrived like this."

In unison, they replied, "Yes."

"Just like this? You opened the box, and the air conditioner was like this?"

Mike said, "Yes," and Justin coughed.

Ms. Becker tried to continue with, "So you did not place the air conditioner in the window and..."

Mike said a bit too loudly, "No!" Then he softened his tone a bit. "Um, what? Ah, no. You see, why would we place the clearly destroyed air conditioner in the window?"

"And I have this cough, you see," Justin said, "so I couldn't help put it in the window."

Mike sharply turned his head directly to Justin B. Hayford.

"Yes, and thank you, Justin, even though we didn't even try to put the air conditioner in the window anyway."

"Because of my cough."

"No, Justin, no. Your cough had nothing to do with the way this air conditioner arrived. Please stop talking about your cough."

Justin then coughed.

Ms. Becker continued, but first, she placed her tongue on the top of her front teeth under her lip and made a smacking noise.

"So, you boys want me to believe that you opened this box, with just a dent on each corner of it, and found, encased in these foam pieces, this completely flattened air conditioner?"

Mike, not sure of what to do next, whispered to Justin, "If you cough, I will kill you."

"Ms. Becker," Mike continued, "Ms. Becker..." And then Mike began to cry. Real fake, forced tears flowed. Mike was crying as if he had put Vick's VapoRub right onto his eyeballs. Mike repeated, "It happened! It truly happened. For the love of God, it happened!" And Mike fell on the box, weeping quietly into the foam peanuts, repeating over and over, "It happened. It happened. It happened."

Ms. Becker said, "Yeah, okay. I get it. I've had a very long morning. I'm not in a terrific mood...but this is the best story I've seen or heard anyone try to pull off. And I admit, I am truly impressed with your dedication to this story. And the cough. That's a terrific cough. And so, I'm just going to go with it. Damage report finished. Your father will be reimbursed for the appliance and for the shipping."

Mike rose to his feet. Justin just stood there.

"Thank you, Ms. Becker."

"Yeah...no...don't thank me. This whole extravaganza was better than the 3:00 P.M. *Big* movie on Channel 6." She turned to leave. Then she stopped and said, "You know, that extension cord is a bit of overkill, don't you think? Take care of that cough. And by the way, the cough didn't cover up the kicking all that much. Have a nice day."

And she left, laughing the whole way down the hallway.

Mike closed the door to the studio and said, "That took a lot out of me."

Justin said, "That was some of your best work. And I do think the cough helped."

CHAPTER 14

I can't remember the exact date, but I remember that a popular song at the time was "When Doves Cry" by Prince and the Revolution. I always liked that song.

I guess we could call this "The Summer of Justin B. Hayford." That summer, Justin came to live with Mike in that small apartment with that stupid window, and that even more stupid air conditioner.

The air conditioner wasn't the only scathing idea Mike and Justin experienced together that summer. Mike had tons of those scathing ideas. All of which started as innocently as him adding the baking soda and vinegar to his third-grade volcano experiment, and I can safely say, most of those ideas ended up with the same intense reaction. I think some of Mike's best qualities were his spontaneity and love of a good caper.

So. "The Summer of Justin B. Hayford." Here we go.

It all began with George Eastman, the man who invented the Brownie camera and, along with Kodak, launched personal picture-making and jump-started the filmmaking industry that it is today. Now, that may seem like a large jump back in time, but this story takes place not with George Eastman in 1930, but at his mansion in the early 1980s. Yes, George Eastman had an absolutely exquisite Georgian mansion on East Avenue in New York State. Ironically enough, one of Justin and Mike's friends was Bea Doran. Bea was a nighttime security guard at the Eastman mansion on the very famous East Avenue in that very famous state.

The story has already taken an odd turn because anyone who is friends with Justin or Mike could not possibly be qualified to be a security guard of a billion-dollar industry home and archive. I digress, but I also believe since absolutely no one was interested in breaking into the George Eastman House, being a security guard there was not a difficult job. People didn't realize that most film archives from the first films ever made up through to the mid-1950s were logged in, categorized, and stored in the American Theater Film wing and the Foreign Film wing of this mansion.

Bea was a really fun person to be with, and she often invited Justin and Mike to enjoy all the pleasures of the mansion and help her be a security guard. Basically, Bea was bored and just wanted the company. This mansion was exquisite. The films they watched were amazing. To see Louise Brooks' screen test, Mabel Normand's first film, Joan Crawford's screen test... Truly amazing.

The mansion was also like the game of Clue. The rooms, like the dining room, vast and dark, came to life in magnificent form from the game itself. There was even a conservatory. There was an amazing ballroom with two marble staircases winding their way to the second-floor bathroom. There was even a barber shop.

There was George Eastman's handwritten letter that he left on his desk in his bedroom stating, "My work is done," and then he shot himself in the head. Mike thought at least they knew it was George Eastman with a gun in his bedroom by the desk and not Professor Plum with a candlestick or Miss Scarlet with the rope. There wasn't a Colonel Mustard. There was, however, Grey Poupon mustard in the fridge.

There was an antique revolver, an eccentric billionaire, and a rather modest bedroom for someone so rich. Bea and Mike could not get over that Eastman slept in a double bed. If he was so rich, why didn't he sleep in a king-size bed? Did they have king-size beds back then? Why was his closet so small? Oh, they bet George Eastman regretted killing himself back then when he could've held on just a few more years and have a king-size bed and a bathroom right in his room before deciding to kill himself later on in the century.

I digress again, and I apologize. Souls usually don't digress. But I need to lay the groundwork here.

Justin was also an aspiring filmmaker. He always had a filmmaking camera stuck to his eye, always. Over the course of one summer, Justin and Mike visited Bea at the George Eastman house numerous times. They would sit in the kitchen having coffee and talk about making a murder mystery film at the George Eastman House after hours when no one was around. I know you're wondering about security cameras and other people looking in. You would think there would be these things; there wasn't. It was a time when you just hired a security guard, and their job didn't include videotapes or anything to be reviewed later. This made it easy for Justin to live his dream of making a murder mystery in the George Eastman House on East Avenue in New York State a reality.

What was the premise? Well, let's just say Justin wasn't the next Martin Scorsese of the filmmaking industry— especially in *Super 8* style. But he was a free thinker. Justin wrote a film called *Bozo's Fun Has Just Begun*. I'll repeat that because I'm sure you think you didn't read it correctly. The name of the film was *Bozo's* (as in the clown) *Fun Has Just Begun* (as in murder).

Bad? Ummm...well... It's very complicated. Bozo invites celebrities who have wronged him over the years to his amazing mansion and kills them off, one by one. Not the most original script but clearly a new take on the subject. Mike played the Queen of England—no surprise there. Mike, Justin, and Bea enlisted their friends to play other roles, and their scathingly brilliant idea was to have all arrive at the George Eastman House on East Avenue in New York State at 2:00 A.M. This would ensure that no one else would be there, and the plan was for all to be done and gone by 6:30 A.M., as the next shift would begin at 8:00 A.M.

Andy was going to play the Prime Minister of Canada. Cousin Donna was to play Mother Burnside from the Jerry Herman musical *Mame*. (Don't ask about that one as no one really understood it.) Donna may have stolen her costume when she played that role in *Mame*, and it was just a good costume to have for the film. Patty was going to play glamorous film star, Louise Brooks. Bozo was being played by Bea. Now, just to be further irritating, Justin B. Hayford made everyone in the film call Bozo, Bozo T. Clown. Eye-rolls around the room.

Everyone arrived, and it was a really fun and exciting night. They felt like they were doing something illegal and at the same time legal (but, was it?). It also felt like a cool way to bond and have a memorable experience together. Yes, it was all these things.

Now, remember: This is one of Mike's "scathingly brilliant" ideas. So, now let me tell you how memorable the experience became.

Everything was rehearsed, and Mike, as the Queen of England, fell down the flight of stairs, breaking her neck and dying. Mike was really good at this. He had this idea that he would have a close-up on his eyes as he/she looked left to right. Then the film would cut to his/her patent leather clutch, and the clutch would close shut sharply. And then it would cut to his/her shoulders being thrust forward by clown hands, and then Mike did this amazing stunt man fall down this winding flight of stairs, and he/she died at the bottom—all while applying red lipstick and aerating Chanel #5 on his/her neck. It was genius.

Cousin Donna "died" around the fountain in the mansion's conservatory, remarking in a thick southern accent "how cool the watuhh" felt around her wrists. Then she was drowned to death by a clown hand. Patty, as Louise Brooks, died during a bob-styled haircut. Yes, they did use George Eastman's very own barbershop chair. And, of course, the scissors were held by Bozo T. Clown's hand.

So, with all the death shots out of the way, and it now around 4:00 A.M., the only shots left were everybody's arrival at the front door, which was very easy. And then there was the banquet shot where everyone sits in the grand dining room around an amazing table, using all of George Eastman's China, silverware, and gold trimmed glasses. All the players were seated, and Bozo T. Clown arrived late to the dinner and then explained to everyone that one by one, he would kill them for various reasons. Everything was going along just fine—sounds normal to me...until Mike had another scathingly brilliant idea.

For some reason, Mike had it in his head that the original Rembrandt painting (yes, an original) that hung above the credenza in the dining room, clearly costing well into the millions of dollars, could somehow get destroyed in all the mayhem of this film shoot. No one was really worried about the million dollars' worth of China, or glass, or silverware, or gold trimmed glasses, but Mike was very concerned about that Rembrandt.

If they were so worried, wouldn't a normal person just take the Rembrandt off the wall and store it somewhere safe in the mansion and then put the Rembrandt back on the wall when everything was cleaned up and safe? This would be the normal thing to do. Another normal thing to do is to not move the Rembrandt and film it anyway and make sure no one touches said priceless Rembrandt. Normal people would do that. These people were filming a show about Bozo the Clown killing everyone. These people were not normal. Clearly.

So, Mike's brilliant idea was he thought it best if they took the Rembrandt off the wall and put it into the empty trunk of his mother's 1981 Traverse engine K Car parked in the driveway. That way, the painting could be locked in the trunk, and no one could get to it, and it would be safe. First of all, the K Car was never actually all that safe. I don't mean to mock the K Car by Chrysler, but the K Car wasn't the safest car.

Amazingly, everyone agreed this was the best plan. So, they gingerly took the Rembrandt off the wall and placed it into Mike's mom's K Car trunk. They all went back inside and finished up shooting this giant banquet, finishing around 7:00 A.M.

They were running late with a lot of cleanup to do to get this mansion back to looking as if absolutely nothing happened this one long night in the middle of summer. There was a frenzy of activity. They had to clean up the lipstick from the Queen of England, they had to clean up fake blood, they had to clean up the kitchen where they were eating, they had to clean up the banquet room, so it looked like no one ever had a banquet...

It was daunting. Bea reminded everybody that it was 7:45 A.M., and her replacement would be coming very soon. Everyone looked at each other, pleased with their adventure and their deft cleaning skills. Everything was done, so everyone raced out the door to their cars and drove away.

Yes, you guessed it...Mike drove away with the Rembrandt in the trunk of the disaster of a car known as the K Car. Yup! Everyone got home, very self-satisfied and excited that they made this film. Everyone was glowing, basking warmly in the moment...including Mike. Then Mike turned on the television to watch reruns of *The Dick Van Dyke Show*, or commonly known in the Pennello family as "The Penis Van Lesbian Show." There was a news report interrupting "The Penis Van Lesbian Show." It was something about a missing painting at the George Eastman House on East Avenue in New York State.

Mike almost threw up on his shoes.

The newscast switched to the security guard. It was Bea! She was saying it was just a normal night there at the George Eastman House on East Avenue in New York State. She did her security check rounds as usual, and there was no sign of anyone or any intrusion or alarms going off. Well, it was a debacle. Seconds later, the phone rang, and he heard the whispered hush of Bea.

"Mike!"

"Bea!"

"You have got to get this painting back to this house!"

"Bea, it's not a house; it's a mansion."

"Okay, fine. Yes, you have to get the Rembrandt back to the mansion! I don't know how else to explain this except the truth. And no one would believe the 'truth' that we were making a film about a clown killing the Queen of England."

"Good point. What's the plan? My mom took the car to work at the JC Penny Catalogue Department Store at Culver Ridge."

"Mike, I know where your mom works. I don't care about that right now. I'm doing a really good job of holding them off the trail, but they're saying that it was some sort of very in-depth and calculated heist, and they think I could not have any idea what's happening—kind of like a museum heist. I've been a security guard here for eight years, and they trust me implicitly. But, I gotta tell you, Mike, you basically stole a priceless Rembrandt, and now it's sitting in the trunk of a K Car in the parking lot of a JCPenney Catalogue store." Bea paused for a beat, then said, "I don't know what's worse...that you stole a Rembrandt or that your mother drives a K Car. In any case, get that Rembrandt back to this mansion somehow."

With Bea still on the line, Mike thought for a moment then said, "Okay, here's a plan."

Bea said, "Oh, no. Not another plan...and please, I can't have another Bozo T. Clown plan. I literally just sat in through a police interview where they asked me about some white paint or makeup on the doorknob. Luckily, I said that I use the white make up to highlight my under eyes because I tend to have dark circles because of the late hours I work. Luckily this policeman was an idiot and believed it."

Mike said, "Well, you do have dark circles under your eyes."

"That is not the point. And ouch, by the way. You have to get that Rembrandt painting back here somehow, or everything is going to go tits up!"

And then she hung up the phone. Mike had never heard the expression "tits up," but he thought perhaps it was not good.

Then the telephone calls started rolling in. All the friends called to say, "What are we gonna do—what do we do—what should we do—what are we gonna do?" Clearly, everyone wanted to know what they were going to do.

Finally, Mike said, "Here's what we are going to do. We're going to go back tonight. We're going to repeat the whole thing. We're gonna go back at 2:00 a.m . We are going to hang that picture—" (how cute...he called a priceless Rembrandt painting a "picture") "...right back up where it belongs. And then we're going to leave. And everything will be well."

Everyone was impressed with his calm and thought this sounded like a solid plan.

Interestingly, no one thought that there would be extra security guards on that night or that there might be a police car watching the George Eastman House mansion on East Avenue in New York State, but nonetheless, that was the plan. Mike called Bea and told her the plan. Oddly enough, Bea said that she would be the only security guard on that night, but security guards would be popping in and out to check in with her but not starting until 3:00 A.M. Bea agreed to proceed with the plan.

Justin was very excited because he wanted to film the whole thing, creating a film entitled *The Un-heisting*. Mike said to Justin that if he filmed one second of this, he would crack his camera over his head until he was dead. Then the Rembrandt would be back in place, and there would be a dead body under it. Then he would be blamed for stealing the Rembrandt, killing himself for feeling guilty about stealing it in the first place, thus bringing shame to his lovely Protestant Hayford family in Irondequoit, New York. Justin agreed to these terms.

The plan went like clockwork. They were in and out of the mansion like *Mission Impossible*. Or was it "Mansion Impossible"? They had developed a series of calls and responses to make sure no other security guards were around. Bea would beam her flashlight in the main ballroom on the main floor to signal that no one else was there and that it would be okay to enter from the back street up to the main house and put the Rembrandt back on the wall.

The Rembrandt was back. Everyone was home. Everyone turned on the TV, and there it was—the unexplainable return of the Rembrandt to the George Eastman House on East Avenue in New York State. No investigator could figure out how it had been stolen; no investigator could figure out how it had been returned.

The last line of the news story was Bea saying, "I just prayed that the Lord would help with the return of this painting and that no one would get hurt. I prayed that the stupid clown—" she then looked more directly into the camera, "...clowns—who had the nerve to steal that painting in the first place, were given God's grace of remorse. Thus, returning the hundreds of millions of dollars' worth of a painting that is once again hanging in its place above the Louis VIII credenza."

Mike was very impressed with Bea's statement. She must have practiced it a very long time. He was a little offended she called them all clowns; Mike was clearly playing the Queen of England.

Oh, there are plenty of other "The Summer of Justin B. Hayford" scathingly brilliant idea stories, but here's a simple one I always enjoyed. There was a revival of *Bye Bye Birdie* playing at the Martin Beck Theater. Mike and Justin got it in their sweet, unique heads to paint over the words *Bye Bye Birdie* on the theater's fresh marquee, changing the words to "Poi Poi Pippio" in the middle of the night with many different colors.

They chuckled to think that people arriving for the preview or, especially the cast and producers of *Bye Bye Birdie* would be very confused to see they were buying tickets to "Poi Poi Pippio," starring Donald O'Connor and Chita Rivera.

The show was a total flop, but Justin and Mike didn't think it had anything to do with the marquee. It was just a bad show.

CHAPTER 15

I am now seated in the vinyl chair in the room, looking at Mike. This chair is periwinkle blue and ugly. It's the same color as Mrs. Terrani's ranch-style house on the corner of Echo Street and Cascade Place. Why did she paint her house that color that everyone had to see? It's like you can't not see periwinkle. Anyway, the chair...it was ugly and oddly comfortable. Mike looks the same. The cord feels the same. Same, same, same.

You know, I have to agree with Mike on that whole dissertation thing. If you have a moment, please do look at Busby Berkeley films. He does turn people into machine-like formations. I just can't get it off my mind. Mike's thesis was pretty good. In fact, five years after Mike graduated, Manhattan College asked him to be the keynote speaker at a School of Journalism event. Mike was kind and supportive, but gave a solid hard jab at the cheap Rosalind Russell look-alike, Dean Francis Broderick, and her rather unfortunate choice about giving the A to Kelly Ryan. Mike felt vindicated.

The nurse comes into Mike's room again, puts some red roses on the bedside table, and leaves. Someone in another room probably passed and didn't need them anymore. That was nice.

The room becomes much darker now. It feels like there are less than 12 hours left. This can be looked at in one of two ways. One: Imagine watching your least favorite aunt die for 12 hours and how daunting that can be. Two: And now think you're a non-being with all the time in the world, and you have 12 hours to reminisce with your person who you liked. It's all relative.

Speaking of relatives...

So, let's see...you know about Rose, Del, Sal, Maria, Gloria, Connie, Cecelia, Jim-Lenny-Zeke, Augie, Johnny, Angelina, Jenny, and Nancy. Let's move on. Pauline...enough said. Do you know any Paulines who don't act like a "Pauline"? Name a girl Pauline, and you will end up with a largish type woman who loves sports. Not in every case, but in every case in Mike's family. Aunt Angie...walking perfection with gorgeous snow-white hair and who made broccoli taste good to a child. This was an accomplishment. Aunt Angie somehow worked a miracle with that broccoli. You should try it, but she's been dead for over 100 years. It wouldn't taste right.

Aunt Gene. She was fun and dynamic. Aunt Gene loved everyone and was warm and welcoming. Aunt JoJo. Beautiful, smart, loving, giving, perfect, had an advanced sense of humor, a doctorate, and never acted haughtily. She was one of Rose's five sisters. Aunt Rose. Just so you know, there are eight Aunt Roses. There is the bowler, the card player, the loud one, the patent leather purse one, the $5 at Christmas one, the one from Brooklyn, the mourner, and the slow one.

By the way, anyone in the entire family, even if they married in, could, at any given moment, slap you for doing something wrong. And no one questioned it. Here is an example.

> *Mike runs into the kitchen while his mother Maria is preparing eggplant.*
> *"Ma! Aunt Connie just slapped me, and I lost a tooth."*
> *"What did you do?"*
> *"Nothing. It was Johnny."*
> *"Well, remember that for the next time and stay outta trouble."*
> *"Ma, I didn't do anything. It was Johnny."*
> *"Were you with Johnny?"*
> *"Yes, but like at the other side of the room."*
> *"Did you watch Johnny?"*
> *"Yeah, but I didn't know what he was doing."*
> *"It's the same thing, and you shoulda been slapped."*
> *"But Johnny didn't get slapped."*
> *Maria stopped slicing and looked up from the eggplant.*
> *"Sal! Sal!" she screamed. "You goddamn son-of-a-bitch, come up from the cellar, and come up here to the kitchen."*

Sal yelled up from the basement.

"I'm fixin' a leak down here, Maria."

"Now? Now you decide to fix the leak? Now, when I have something to tell you? I've been asking you to fix that leak for a year. Now you fix it?"

"Maria, who the hell cares when I fix it? I'm fixing it now."

Mike, thinking the topic needs to get back on track, says, "Ma...I lost a tooth."

"Shut up, you whiney son-of-a-bitch. Sal, come upstairs, go up and find Johnny, and slap him."

"Why?"

"Why? You wanna know why, Sal? Because if you don't go slap Johnny, I'm coming down there, and I am gonna kick you in the nuts."

"Ma...my tooth."

"Go to hell, Mikey."

Sal said, "Jesus Christ and the whole Holy Family, I'll be right up."

Sal enters the kitchen.

"What did Johnny do?"

Sal sees Mikey.

"Did Johnny knock out Mikey's tooth? I'll go slap him."

Maria interrupts, "No. Connie slapped Mikey."

"Maria, I can't go slap Connie."

"No...go slap Johnny."

"Oh. For what?"

"Johnny did something."

"What did he do?"

"I don't know."

"Okay, I'll go slap him."

Sal walks away, yelling up the stairs, "Johnny, I'm coming up to slap you, and I don't know why, but you will be slapped. Connie, I'm coming up to slap your son, Johnny."

Aunt Connie says, "Nobody gives a shit, Sal."

Mike says, "Thanks, Ma."

Maria says, "And you get out of my sight before I slap you for just being here while I am busy trying to press the acid out of this eggplant."

Chapter 16

Including the slapping, there were rules of being a Pennello. Well, really, the rules of being Italian.

Kiss everyone in the room, even if you don't know them.

If something in the refrigerator has cling wrap on it and aluminum foil over the cling wrap, do not touch it. It's for some unknown party somewhere.

If anyone tells you to get their purse, get it. And let me tell you: Every lady over at the family complex had a purse you had to get. What was in there? My God!

If you have bad news or need to say something so only the right people hear it, sing it lightly. Check out the movie *Moonstruck* for the truth here. Hint: "It's Johnny Camerari."

Whisper all diseases.

Visit everyone who goes into the hospital, even if they just deliver your newspaper.

You must like Frank Sinatra. Personally, Mike thought Frank was a little pitchy, but a genius of phrasing. But don't ever say you don't like Frank Sinatra. And if you mention Connie Francis, someone in the room will say, "You know she got attacked in a hotel room. Oh, it was awful."

Swearing is not really a thing in an Italian home. Here's an example: "You goddamn son-of-a-bitch, get down here right now." That's just means it's dinner time.

Sometimes, an aunt loved you so much she slapped you, which left you confused.

Salad is last in the meal.

"*You wanna know why, Mikey?*" *asked Uncle Tony at every holiday meal.*

"*Not really, Uncle Tony.*"

"*Because the salad is the least digestible food. If you eat the salad first, your stomach can't break it down, and then all the other food you eat sits on top of the salad, and you bloat.*"

"*Okay.*"

"*You'll bloat, Mikey! You will bloat!*"

"*I got it.*"

"*Good. Don't bloat, Mikey. You don't wanna bloat, Mikey, right?*"

"*No one wants to bloat, Uncle Tony.*"

If it's a holiday, expect to visit all the relatives on an endless car trip in the morning even if they are coming over to the house three hours later.

At the end of dinner, if you're a man, you play cards, and if you're a woman, you wash the dishes. If you're gay, you pray *Easter Parade* is on TV and watch it upstairs.

Now, the above sounds unequal. And it is. But the women in Mike's family actually enjoyed getting away from their stupid husbands, so they could have some time together to bash them and laugh about them without the idiots they married being around.

CHAPTER 17

Mike always said he was bored. I don't know how boring feels though. Time will always be time, and how it is spent will always just be spent. As a Soul, I know there is no time, so there was no real thinking about time for me, but Mike thought about it a lot. He didn't have the knowledge that time is an endless stream of events and non-events that just become a collective. It all becomes part of a giant non-library, keeping all the moments of all the moments of the world.

Why I am thinking this, I don't know. But I've noticed that the sounds on the machines hooked up to Mike seem to be going as anyone would expect them to be going right now. I don't know if the room is cold or hot because I don't have those feelings or sensors in the skin, but Mike seems comfortable enough. If his mother were alive and here, she'd be putting an extra blanket on him, for sure.

I like thinking about Mike's family more than anything in the world. They were a mix of the craziest and most loving people I have ever experienced. They were such a dichotomy and could swing 180 degrees in less than a second. They did not need psychological help; it's just that they were so passionate about everything. Whether President Kennedy got shot or Grandma couldn't find *Falcon Crest* on the TV carried the same amount of weight. It was amazing. Mike loved his family very much. And the family depended on him for much. Mike had to be the entertainer. He had to be the most fun at every party. Mike had to be the show that was never produced, written, or rehearsed, but expected. And Mike liked this job because no one else could do this job in the family.

Yes, Mike loved his family deeply, but there was one person in the family that Mike never really liked. It was Gramps. Gramps was on his mother's side. The entire family loved Gramps, but Mike knew a different side of him. The whole family thought Gramps was the most kind, generous, and gracious person in the entire family. However, they didn't have a room next to Gramps and Grandma Rose. Mike got to hear the horrible things Gramps would say to Rose and the horrible treatment that Gramps gave her. Gramps, on the outside, was a kindly family man. Inside their bedroom, he was an awful condescending, abusive jerk. No, not a jerk. No, he was a selfish, narcissistic abuser.

The feeling was mutual, and Mike knew that Gramps didn't like him. Gramps did, however, worship Gloria, Mike's sister. For some reason, Gramps held Gloria in the palm of his hand. There's an actual photograph to prove that it was literally true. Gramps held Gloria in the palm of his hand, his pride, his gold medal, his goddess, like the most important person in his life. Mike had absolutely no jealousy about this. Gloria didn't ask to be held in the palm of everyone's hand because Gloria was one of the kindest people on Earth. Mike was happy that at least one of them was liked by Gramps.

Mike knew that Gramps was fighting his own demons. He remembered hearing snippets of stories about Gramps and an incident in a Catholic school and maybe an unfortunate incident with the priest. As the youngest of 10 children, Gramps always got a lot of attention and never had to do anything. When he got married, he had to actually do something for himself and his family. That was something he was not used to, as his older siblings had done everything for him. And when he married Rose, he had to get a job and actually do something. But the truth of the matter wasn't that Gramps was never able to hold a job, get a job, or finish anything.

He did manage to destroy his young grandson, Mike. Early on in Mike's life, Gramps would always make it a point to somehow make Mike feel bad about anything he did. But this was always done in the privacy of just him and Mike. As I said, Gramps was loved by everyone and remembered to be "so kind and loving."

Mike only remembered his bedroom door opening in the middle of the night when he was little, and Gramps would be standing next to his bed, whispering in his ear, "You act like a girl in front of everybody, and you're an embarrassment to the family. You shouldn't have been born. You're a girl." This would happen at least twice a week.

When Mike would be having a birthday party with his friends over to the house, he and his friends would often be in the pool as Mike's birthday was during the early summer. Gramps would yell out of the second-story window at Mike, "You swim like a girl, and you're embarrassing your whole family." This would happen in front of his friends. If Mike had to pick one, his "favorite" Gramps moment was when he was cutting the lawn. Gramps would take the time and effort to walk outside and yell over the din of the lawnmower, "You cut the lawn like a girl." Although it hurt Mike, his defense mechanism of sharp wit made him think to himself, *How does a girl cutting the lawn differ from a boy cutting the lawn?* Maybe it was the cork clogs, hot pants, and sparkle tube top Mike was wearing while cutting the lawn that made Gramps say it...not sure.

Mike never showed that he was fazed too much by this abuse. And everyone living in the same house did not seem to notice this abuse at all. Mike also thought too much of his parents and sister to even bring it up, so he just sucked it up. Things went on like this, and Mike became very callous to this treatment. He knew he would end up going away to college, and away from this man where he wouldn't have to deal with it.

Sometimes Mike wondered if his mother was ever treated this way by Gramps, her own father. But based on how he treated Gloria, he suspected that she received the same kind of doting love. Mike was sure it was just him and that he was not able to be the "man" that Gramps thought a man should be. And while Mike did deeply suppress this and live with it, almost ignoring it, it did make him hate Gramps.

I have to smile now as Mike got his great revenge. This is perhaps the best story of Mike's life. It was almost out of a Bette Davis movie. No, it was better than a Bette Davis movie.

Mike was living in Midtown Manhattan, and the phone rang, and it was the "Mom voice" that she made when there was terrible news. It always started with: "Mike, how are you? That's good. What are you doing; is it a bad time?" Mike knew this could only be one thing— the death call.

"Ma, who died?"

"No one...yet. Your grandfather is in the hospital and is not expected to do well."

Mike was nonplussed by this. But he did try to feign concern for the sake of his mom.

"What's wrong?"

"Your grandfather had a stroke, he's lost his speech, and he's probably not going to come out of it, so you should probably come home. You should get on the train and come home."

Mike said, "Okay," and he packed a light bag, and he got on the train and headed home for whatever was going to happen. Mike did not feel sad. He was more concerned about Grandma Rose and his mother than his grandfather having a stroke and being in the hospital.

Mike arrived home, and it was almost as if the wake was already happening. Grandma Rose was crying; his mom was crying; his dad was pacing, and Gloria was up in her room listening to Stevie Nicks. The whole family and every apartment in the building was very concerned, and each would take turns yelling down from the staircase every five minutes: "Is there any news from the hospital?" This was literally every five minutes, and Mike had had enough. He suddenly had an idea.

Mike brought the whole family together and asked if each member of the family had a chance to visit Grandpa in the hospital. Each said yes that they did go visit. Mom said that she would be there now, but he looked stable for the night, and so she came home. Mike said, "You know, I think I should go and visit Gramps because I am the only one that hasn't gotten a chance to say hello."

Mom reminded Mike that it was not visiting hours. Mike said that he would take his chances. Everyone was so proud of Mike to venture out and try to see his grandfather, who might not make it through the night. Little did they know.

So Mike took the train to St. Mary's Hospital, the same hospital he was born in. He went up to the wing that was for geriatric patients in critical but stable condition. The hospital elevator doors opened, and the hallway was very dim. Mike saw just a few overhead fluorescent lights and, in the distance, the nursing station that was staffed by only one nurse...a desk lamp shining brightly, making her face glow. Mike thought she looked like an Angel, but an Angel in a Stephen King novel. Mike walked over to the nursing station, and he whispered, "Hello. I am Mike Pennello. My grandfather is here with a stroke, and I've been away, and I haven't had a chance to see him."

The nurse quickly snapped and said visiting hours were over and to come back in the morning.

Mike knew exactly what he had to do.

Mike turned on "the actor." He turned on the Matthew Broderick in *Biloxi Blues*. Mike could turn on Jimmy Stewart combined with Olivia de Havilland, with just a hint of Joan Crawford when she could actually be endearing, if he needed to.

Mike told the nurse that he realized the visiting hours were over, but he had just heard the news about his favorite grandfather having a stroke. He took in a deep dramatic breath and continued that everyone else in the family has had their chance to see him. Mike said that he would never be able to live with himself if he didn't try to tell his grandfather how much he loved him before he went.

Mike said, "You see, nurse...things like this only happen once, and you look like you've seen your share of pain. I don't know if Gramps will be alive in the morning. I know this is a lot to ask, and I can only ask you once. You can see my eyes are full of tears, and my heart is even more full of sadness. I wonder if you would be willing to, just this once, break the rules and let me go visit my Gramps for what might be the last time. Please, nurse. You will not even know I'm here. I will just simply walk into the room and whisper to him just a few words. I promise it'll be just a few words. And then I will make my exit past your desk, and you will know you have done me a great service. I'm a good boy, nurse. I am a good boy."

Even Mike thought that last part about being a "good boy" was a bit over the top, but it worked. The nurse told him the room number and said something about how sweet and heartwarming he was. She told him he was the wonderful grandson and that she had never heard a story that touched her so, and that no one would be hurt by her breaking with such a silly rule anyway. Mike thanked her and walked towards Gramps's room.

He opened the door to the room. It was dark. It was dark because it was night. There was only the glow of the lights on Gramps from the machines keeping him alive. It was glowing enough to see the shape of his grandfather's body. The blinds were drawn, and the room was a little bit surreal.

Mike flipped the light switch on in the room, lighting it up like a bowling alley with fluorescent lights overhead. Mike cleared his throat—loudly. He could see Gramps slowly awake, and then as Gramps recognized Mike, he began to sit up in bed. Gramps seemed to smile...happy to see Mike. The feeling was not mutual. And then the Bette Davis scene began. Here's what Mike said, verbatim:

"How perfect. How perfect that there you are, lying in bed, unable to speak when all you had to say to me my whole life were words of hate and abuse. How perfect for you. And how perfect for me. And how pathetic you look, just lying there, unable to abuse me or even your wife. How perfectly life works out for all of us. Oh, you thought I was coming to say hello and how much I loved you. Well, I didn't. I came to say it looks like you're dying like a little girl, and you're an embarrassment to the whole family."

Gramps's face became knotted and strained. He fell back on the bed as the machines flat-lined. Mike simply turned off the overhead fluorescent lights, opened the door, walked out into the hallway, and closed the door gently.

And as he walked past the nurses' station, he said, "You have no idea how much that meant to me."

CHAPTER 18

I t's 1985 and a banner year. Mike was cast in a Broadway National Tour
of a major musical about a redheaded child hiding from her mean war-
den and hoping for adoption by a millionaire. I know you're thinking, "I
don't recall a musical version of *The Diary of Anne Frank*." *Annie* was
fantastic, and Mike did five years of that show. It was massive and lush
and expensive, and Mike made more money than he ever thought possible. He thought about Kelly Ryan and wondered how her cigarette habit
was going.

Mike had all the funny roles in the show and eventually became the
dance captain and finally the Director's Assistant. At contract time in year
three, Mike did not ask for a raise like everyone usually does. Mike asked
for someone to carry his luggage. No extra money, just a person to pick up
his luggage outside his hotel room, load it on the truck or bus, or check-in
at the airport, and deliver the luggage to the new hotel room. The producers
gladly granted the request. You have no idea how difficult it is to be con-
tinually carrying your luggage after three years on the road.

In year four of the *Annie* tour, Mike asked for new luggage. The producers gave him a raise and also made him the Resident Director of the
show. Mike really wanted new luggage, but he accepted the deal anyway.
Mike enjoyed this new role. He loved the casting and rehearsal process,
and he was good at it. One contract cycle, Mike cast this beautiful woman
named Denise in the role of Grace Farrell. Denise was perfect for the part
and had lovely brunette hair.

Now, hair doesn't matter because every woman in the show and a few men were given wigs. The role of Grace is always blonde. Always. Mike changed that and said that Denise's hair color was so lovely and was gorgeous against her skin tone that her wig should be brunette. And, so it was. As is always part of the rehearsal period, the cast went to "designer run-through." This is when the original creative and technical staff return and make sure the work is still the top-notch Tony Award-winning show it always was.

The run-through was going great. Grace Farrell walked into Miss Hannigan's room to find Annie, and the costume designer, Theoni V. Aldredge, stood up in the middle of The Ambassador Theater and screamed, "Stop this horrendous offense."

Everyone stopped.

Theoni continued, "How dare you, Mike Pennello! How dare you! Martin Charnin would roll over in his grave!"

"I'm right here," said Martin Charnin. Geez...no one noticed he showed up.

Mike said, "Umm...something wrong, Theoni?"

"Oh, I know your little game, Mike."

"Canasta?"

"Oh, please, Michael. Don't be funny, charming, and coy; you ladder climber you. That ladder goes nowhere for you. I have a Tony Award for the design of this show. I have created each costume to enhance, explore, exemplify, and...and..." She ran out of words that began with "E." "...and help bring life to each character. And Grace Farrell is blonde. She looks like hell in this green suit for this first scene."

Theoni began to walk down the aisle towards the stage: "She will look worse in the powder blue flowing dress in the Warbucks Mansion when she sings that awkward little song about cheese. Sorry, Martin."

"That was Strouse," said Martin.

Theoni was now on stage next to poor Denise: "And she will look like hell in the gorgeous black gown in the finale. Do you want to look horrible...what's your name, sweetheart?"

Denise said, "Denise."

"Denise? Are you sure?"

"I was until now. Yes. It's Denise Mathers."

Pulling her head back to get a better look at Denise, she said, "Unfortunate. You should change that to Denise Matthews. That has a better ring to it."

Denise said, "I will get right on that, Ms. Aldredge."

"Do you want to look horrible, Denise?"

"I'd prefer not to."

"Okay. There you have it, Mike Pennello."

Theoni began to walk downstage towards the lip of the stage.

"I have four Tony Awards..."

Mike yelled out from the audience, "You have three. You still think you won for *Dreamgirls*, but you lost."

Theoni, clearly in a rage, continued her precarious walk downstage.

"I have numerous awards, and I created Grace Farrell to be blonde, and so this wig will be changed to blonde. The color of this wig shall be..."

Theoni fell off the front of the stage and into the orchestra pit. The lights must have been in her eyes.

Mike completed her sentence, "Blonde? Shall we go with blonde, Miss Aldredge?"

A beat goes by.

Theoni, in a muffled and slightly pained voice, manages to get out the word, "Yes."

Annie took Mike to almost every major city in the United States and Canada's one major city. Being part of *Annie* was dreamy, rewarding, and life-changing, and as all shows do, it closed. Mike was always good about change and show closings. He actually couldn't wait for something to change or just be over. Mike always thought rehearsals were awesome and that opening night was great. Then Mike would be good. Done.

Parties. Same. Loved the idea of a party, planning the party, then he'd dread the party was happening, and love it when everyone left.

Relationships. Same. Instant love. Happy times. Fun. Wild romance. One good year. Then, he was over it. The person's breathing would begin to bother him. It's not like it's something easy to change…like slurping. You can say, "Please try to stop slurping." Try, "Hey…can you not breathe?" End of relationship.

So, *Annie* closed, and Mike was fine…and then along came Eva Perón.

CHAPTER 19

People of Argentina...

Mike was cast in *Evita*. One of his favorite shows of all time. It was so slick...so tight...so high to sing. Mike was first tenor and played Eva's brother, Juan Duarte (Juancito). The show was directed by Harold Prince, and Mike was Dance Captain, Swing, and Perón understudy. This is where Mike saw most of Europe and honed his directing craft while being Harold Prince's Assistant Director. It was a critically acclaimed show that changed show business forever and launched a series of documentaries, revivals, and, unfortunately for all people everywhere, a film.

Mike learned the key to direction during this show. Have vision. Stick to it. Listen to good ideas, dissect them to finite ideas, and then use them, unless the ideas are just for change's sake and do nothing for the show's overall theme and function. Mike also learned to speak to a cast as artists who will paint your show with a vivacious life that only a good director can do. He learned that if you just tell people where to stand on stage, you are not a director, you are a dictator...or at best, a mundane traffic cop.

Mike worked show to show, living a life that was fabulous, but alone. Work killed having a life partner. Work. That was what the apartment complex family living taught Mike. You work. How often did Mike hear, "Mike, get the spaghetti number 9 down in the store,"; "Mikey, wash all the floors"; "Mikey, get this fresh pork loin to the Jacobsons"; "Mikey, go to the store and get Grandpa a pack of Pall Malls and a pack of Rolaids."

After being in *Evita* for two years and then being the director for the next four national tours, Mike took a huge departure in his career.

The roller coaster starts now. Please watch your step.

Chapter 20

It's the year 2050, and the number one song on the social unit is "Tipko, Get Off My Snub."

Mike is 89. Good life. Long life. I think there are six hours left. The cord feels about "six hours left" tight.

Just to be clear, I don't have feelings, necessarily. I have memories that make me smile or frown, but I never feel sad or depressed...or happy. I don't need to. I have seen all these feelings in people fade. Souls are made to reflect at the end. Not judge. Not analyze. Not feel. I've never really wondered why I have this job. What's the job? Is it a job? I believe it is a part of life. But, why is a Soul needed? Why can't an Angel do this? Why can't the Source also be the Soul? I have no idea.

Angels, explained already, are sent to fix something for a person. They have an awareness and a sense of self. Angels have a direct link to the Source. They hear the Source and react. They don't debate or converse with the Source. Angels are told, and they go.

The Others pool together, and they hear each Other without words. As I said, the Others don't talk about their persons, but they linger in a tribe of unity. The unity comes from knowing they are the only ones who know that they must energize the body. The Others know their worth, but with no ego at all.

Souls do not have friends, per se. They are all friends, but not friends, a force. You all might like to know that no one goes to Hell or lives in despair for all eternity. I told you earlier but wasn't too specific that you pass on and you join the People. You don't get judged. You are aware if you were a louse or murderer, and you can be sorry about that, but at this point, it doesn't really matter. You also don't go back to be a new person. You just live in a state of calm and numbness.

Okay, so what is all this for then?

No one knows.

There's the Source, the Angels, the Others, the People, and Souls. No matter what they may have turned into now, this is what all religions are built on...actually trying to make it better. May I point out *The Ten Commandments*, *The Story of Ruth*, *The Life of Pi*, *Spartacus*, and *Cats*? All of these strived to make sense of the glory of what lies beyond if you lead a good life. What lies beyond is just...well, the beyond.

Oh...and it is better to try to lead a good life. But it just doesn't really matter.

I ask none of you to go all Bonnie and Clyde and rob banks or go on a killing spree á la *Pulp Fiction* or *Scarface*. Those are just bad choices and wrong...if there is a "wrong" in the grand scheme of things. You can feel free to do non-hurtful stuff. Feel free to spray paint that graffiti on the wall of the abandoned factory though. That's fun.

CHAPTER 21

Five Angels have helped Mike in his life. This is way above average for a musical theater performer.

The first was while Mike was a baby. Maria had a very risky pregnancy in 1961. There was an RH negative factor and stuff I don't understand, and Mary and Sal were told Mike would not make it when born. Maria said the rosary every night of her pregnancy and a special prayer to Saint Gerard, the patron saint of pregnant women. Again, oddly specific. I mean, do we need the word "women" in there? It's kind of a given...but I digress. That's how Mike got the middle name, Gerard, by the way. Angel #1 facilitated Mike's birth with no full blood transfusion needed or death. I kinda had an investment there, too. I chose Mike. It would have been a short stint for me if Mike died.

Another Angel, Angel #2, saved Mike from drowning in his pool when his feet got wrapped tightly, ironically, in the life vest cords.

Angel #3 comes in now. It's 1995. Mike had an audition for *Forbidden Broadway*, a long-running spoof of Broadway shows. In the show, the performers sang parody songs about how Les Miz was so long or how *Miss Saigon* was really just one long song sung for four hours. Mike had a solid audition. He sang "I Got Rhythm," two beats off the rhythm. Honestly, it was hilarious. Go ahead, try it. It's super hard.

When Mike exited the audition, he saw an open audition for a new show at a major theme park across the way. It was to be a musical version of *The Hunchback of Notre Dame*. Mike had a feeling come over him to sign up and audition. Mike fought the feeling. Theme park work?! What? That would be like running the Round-Up at a carnival. It would be like being in an Olde-y Time-y West Show holding up guests with fake guns while riding a horribly decorated stage coach, and you are the bandit. It's worse than being in *Wind and The Willows* at The Marquis Theater on Broadway.

An icy rush entered Mike's body, and a voice said, "Audition." Mike's mind was blown. Not because he received the calling, but he wasn't sure if he heard "tradition" or "audition." Mike decided he heard "audition" and went in the door.

Oh, my God, the room had five people behind a desk, another measuring people, another taking pictures and resumes, and another drawing your footprint. Was Mike getting fitted for a suit or singing two minutes of a song?

A red-faced man said, "Hello."

"I'm Mike. Mike Pennello."

"Welcome to Famous Theme Park auditions for *The Hunchback of Notre Dame*. Can I see your teeth?"

Mike smiled.

Mike heard the table whisper: "Perfect."

Mike said that Mary and Sal paid a lot of money for them.

The red-faced man continued with, "May we measure you?"

"My teeth?"

"No, your height and measurements for costumes."

"Oh. Sure. Will I get to sing?" Mike asked.

"Oh, yes, we do that last."

They finished up the fittings, and then the red-faced man said, "What did you bring to sing today?" Oh, shit. Mike only had off rhythm "I Got Rhythm"...for The Hunchback of Notre Dame! Those two things went together about as well as a chicken dating a dog.

Mike took a breath and began the explanation. "I have 'I Got Rhythm' because I was auditioning next door for *Forbidden Broadway*, and then I came in here.

"Okay...I guess we will hear 'I Got Rhythm.'"

Mike walked over to the accompanist, a very nubby, short, stout, and yet very likable guy.

Mike started, "Do you know...?"

The nubby man piped right in.

"I know 'I Got Rhythm.' Everybody knows, 'I Got Rhythm.'"

Mike tried again.

"Right. Do you generally follow your singers?"

"Umm...yeah... I'm the accompanist."

"Cool. Yes, of course. So, could you—just this once—just keep playing and don't follow me?"

The nubby man said, "I'd love to." Mike started to walk away. The tiny, nubby man said, "Good luck." Then, much louder for the room, "This should be interesting, people."

Well, Mike did the song off rhythm, but dancing on the beat and was funny. Very funny. The room exploded with laughter. The lady outlining people's feet even stopped outlining people's feet.

The laughter died down. Another guy behind the table said, "Do you have anything else?"

Another said again, "He has really nice teeth."

Then another said, "Gorgeous teeth."

This made Mike think, *Did this deformed, deaf hunchback, Quasimodo, have really pretty teeth in this production? What is up with the teeth?*

Mike said no to the question; he didn't have anything else to sing.

"Well, do you know any of our Famous Theme Park songs?"

Mike said, "Yes! I do!"

"Okay, Mike, our accompanist knows pretty much all of our songs, so what would you like to sing?"

"Uptempo or Ballad?"

"Ballad."

Mike thought for a moment and then said, "Ah...okay...How about 'Part of Your World'?"

There was a beat of silence, and a man who looked a bit Latino said, "Umm...usually done by a girl, but actually, in this case, this may be the perfect song for *The Hunchback of Notre Dame*."

Mike thought, *What on Earth kind of musical are they making out of a deformed and deaf boy who dies in a shallow grave? And just might he have fabulous teeth?*

Mike forged on.

"Okay, 'Part of Your World' it is. May I start right at the part after she names all her stuff? She sings about a lot of stuff in the beginning, and I don't think I can remember all her stuff...even though she thinks it's all neat?"

Mike was relieved to hear, "Please do skip the 'stuff' part."

The song went great. Oddly, this song fit Mike's range and ballad quality.

The red-faced man said, "Okay, Mike. That was excellent. You will hear from us in two days if you are under consideration."

Mike said, "Thank you."

"Oh...and by the way," said the red-faced man, "that 'I Got Rhythm' was amazing."

Mike thanked everyone and left the room.

Angel #3 left the room, too.

Chapter 22

M ike was just coming through his apartment door at 314 West 45th Street, fifth floor, when he heard the phone was ringing. Remember, it's 1995. Everyone had landline phones then. Mike picked up the phone and, out of breath, answered with "Hello," but it was a "hello" that sounded like the "hello" his mother made when anyone called at any given time because, at any given time of the day, someone could be calling with the bad news of the death of her kids. Mike and Gloria could be standing right next to Maria, and if the phone rang and she answered it, the "hello" would sound like the police are calling to say Mike and Gloria are dead.

"Hello?"

"Is this Mike Pennello?"

"Yes."

"This is Brenda from Famous Theme Park, and we'd like to offer you a role in *The Hunchback of Notre Dame*."

"Wow! Great! What does this all mean? Is there a callback?"

"No callback. We'd like to offer you the comedic role of one of Quasimodo's gargoyle friends."

"This is based on the Victor Hugo book, right?"

"Yes...with music by a famous person named Alan and lyrics by another famous person named Stephen. Oh, and by the way, your version of 'I've Got Rhythm' has everyone in the Orlando office hysterical. Oh...you were video recorded."

"Umm...cool!?"

So, Brenda went over all the details, the timing, the relocation, the pay, and all the usual stuff. She also asked Mike to think it over for 24 hours and call them back. Mike thanked Brenda profusely and said he would think it over. Mike hung up the phone, and it immediately rang back.

"Hello?" Damn, that same death tone. Damn you, Maria, and your constant thinking someone is dying.

"Hi. Is this Mike Pennello?"

"Brenda?"

"No." (odd pause) "This is Anne Wilson...casting agent for Schecter Scabb. We'd like to offer you a role in *Forbidden Broadway*. The role is Male #2."

Mike sounded very excited.

"Male #2?"

"Yes. Not Male #1."

Mike had no idea which male was 1 or 2 and wasn't sure why he even asked.

Anne went over the details, and Mike said he'd call back with an answer in less than 24 hours. Anne thanked him and said, "That 'I've Got Rhythm' was so stupid fun. It's what got you the job. Talk tomorrow." *Click.*

Mike hadn't even taken his coat off, and he had two offers for work. Every bone in his body said take *Forbidden Broadway* for God's sake. However, there was a gnawing in his stomach that said to definitely go with Hunchback. It was more than a gnawing; it was a calling.

Then Brian walked in the door.

Mike forgot he had a boyfriend. (Not the first time.)

"Hi, Brian."

"Hi, Mike."

Mike asked, "How was your day?"

"Good. Sheri and Donna are coming over with a Christmas tree."

"Why?"

"Because it's Christmastime."

"It's November."

"Yes...Christmastime."

Brian loved the holidays, especially Halloween. He loved Halloween. Mike played along, but he hated Halloween. I think it's because Mike spent his whole life dressed in a costume and to come home just to put on another costume felt like work.

Brian asked, "What are we having for dinner?"

"Well, it sounds like Sheri, Donna, and a Christmas tree."

Brian made a face and said, "I'll order pizza."

"Okay."

Mike continued casually.

"Hey, Brian…I got *Forbidden Broadway* today!"

"What!? Holy cow! That's fantastic. You will be amazing in that show. Wow! Let's celebrate!"

"Yeah! Wee…I also got another offer."

"Really? Wow! What? Not another *Evita*? I don't want you on the road again for a year."

"No. Not *Evita*."

"Okay…what is it?"

"I don't know exactly."

Brian sounded surprised and fearful.

"What?"

"Well, it's at Famous Theme Park playing a leading comedic role in their new musical version of *The Hunchback of Notre Dame*, an animated film that will be coming out in June 1996."

"Is that a set up for a joke?"

"Unfortunately, no."

"New York, though?"

"No."

Brian made a face only Rodin could love for his Gates of Hell.

"God no, not Orlando. Not Orlando. Orlando is like 1972 just hung around and is molding. Orlando smells like someone wiped the whole place down with a musty rag."

Mike decided to keep it all casual.

"Brian, we haven't been to Orlando for years. I think they changed the rag by now. It's only for a year."

"In Orlando, that's like living eight years. Mike, why are you even considering this?"

"I don't know. I have a feeling."

"Wow. A year is a long time." Brian turned away, knowing that this conversation would just spin. "Mike, do what you want. You're gonna anyway."

Brian was right. Mike always did what he wanted, and that was a bit selfish, but Mike was very good about fast analysis, decision-making, and going full throttle. Mike slept on it and decided to go with Hunchback. He surprised Brian with his decision, but himself more. He had one month before his relocation...which sounded odd.

Wouldn't I just do the show and come home?

But, corporate show biz has its own lingo.

Anne from *Forbidden Broadway* was surprised, too. She said, "Theme park. You know that's the death of an actor, right? I mean, it's like a Coney Island sideshow. It's like becoming an old neon sign of a Las Vegas casino that closed in 1966, right? It's like wanting to be on a subway poster about hemorrhoids like that actress Rosalyn Snitow, that is forever branded inside the head of every New Yorker. What's the show?"

"Well, it's a comedy about *The Hunchback of Notre Dame*."

Anne said, "Remember Ishtar," and abruptly hung up the phone.

Mike hung up and then screamed at the phone, "No one remembers Ishtar!"

Then he got what she meant.

Chapter 23

Mike arrived in Orlando wearing ripped black jeans, black boots, a black bomber jacket, and a tight t-shirt. He had to go directly to the Orlando office. They had a very important question for him.

Brenda was waiting for him at her desk.

"Hello, Mike! Welcome. I'm Brenda."

Mike said, "Great to meet you."

Brenda gave Mike the once over.

"Do you normally wear that kind of outfit in all this hot weather?"

Mike wondered if this was the important question.

"Umm...well, it was a lot cooler in NY."

"Of course. That makes sense. We have a little problem here on your medical records we had you fill out before you arrived."

Mike had filled these records out two months ago, and they are just now noticing a medical issue?

"Well...what's the problem?"

"This is silly, really."

"A silly medical problem?"

Brenda cleared her throat.

"Well...here on this questionnaire, it asks if you are blind. Can you see that?"

"Yes. Yes, I can."

"Good...so you're not blind?"

"Um...no."

"Well, you see here, Mike? Where it says are you blind, you checked the box, 'Yes.'"

Mike laughed and said, "I'm not blind, but I definitely just proved that I can't read."

Brenda laughed.

"Ooh, good! That's all, and I'm glad that's all cleared up. We arranged a ride for you to your temporary housing before you find your own permanent residence."

"My permanent residence is in NY. With my boyfriend, Brian."

"Well, we relocate you, and we give you two weeks housing to find where you live for the rest of the year or more of your contract."

"Oh...okay. I must have missed that part. What about transportation to work?"

"Well, your car, of course."

"I'm from NY. We don't have cars."

"You came to Orlando without a car?"

"Yes."

"Well, you can take a bus, but that will take three hours each way. You can rent a car, but really you should buy a car."

"Maybe I can carpool with some of the cast?"

"Well...you can try, but all the schedules don't line up."

"But we all work in the show at the same time."

"There are two full-time casts, and there will be multiple subs, and you never know who you will work with. So, if you have a standing carpool, your schedule may not always align with anyone's schedule. You really should buy a car."

Mike thought for two seconds and then said, "Brenda, you know what? I am blind, and I need to go home. Will you help me find my hat and cane, well not the hat...that just came out because of a dance routine I did once with a hat and cane. I meant dog. Will you help me find my cane and Tippy...the dog, and show me the door? Blind people can't drive."

Brenda laughed and said, "Oh, they all said you were funny...you're funny. Do you know that you're funny?"

Mike had lost his sense of humor.

CHAPTER 24

The next morning Mike woke up in the kitchenette motel room and thought to himself, *Yeah…I'll just go with it.*

For two weeks, he had a driver to take him to rehearsal. He had housing. He had a job in a new musical. He had a gut feeling in the beginning.

A van picked up Mike, along with three other people. A gorgeous girl, a tall blonde male, and a very pretty, comedic actress type.

"Hi! I'm Mike."

"Katie!"

"Colleen!"

"Jeff."

Mike continued, "Cool. I'm playing Hugo, a gargoyle and understudy to Quasimodo."

Katie said she was Esmeralda. Colleen said she was a gargoyle, too, named Laverne. Jeff said he was to be a gargoyle as well, Victor.

Mike put it together. Victor, Hugo, and Laverne. The author's name and then mixed with an homage to Patty, Maxine, and Laverne, The Andrew Sisters!

Okay. That was fun and clever for a musical about a deformed boy who was abused by a cardinal while being held prisoner in a bell tower.

While riding in the van, Mike thought that he could always play the blind card and get out of there if need be. They all arrived at rehearsal, and it looked like a convention was going on. How many people were in this show? There was a table up front, normal, but there were 10 people at that table. Things began. Mike could immediately see that the Stage Manager, Fran, was capable, decisive, and warm. He liked her instantly.

She explained that two full casts were in the room as the show would run seven times a day, seven days a week. Everyone had two days off, so there needed to be two casts. All of a sudden everyone started to look around and size up who their competition would be. Awkward.

Fran showed a map of the theater. It was huge. The theater sat 1,200 people. She shared the set design, and Mike was impressed. Then she showed actual pictures of the theater. Fran said, rather proudly, "...and we added a roof for the audience this year for shade."

Mike died inside. His head and thoughts began to reel. We will be outside? Performing outside is for state fairs and hobo people. And in Florida? This sounded amazingly hot, especially if you were dressed as a gargoyle.

Mike screamed out, "I'm blind!"

First impressions are everything.

Chapter 25

I am sitting on the bed, next to Mike. Mike has a wicked grin on his face. "Blind." So funny. So Mike.

I can imagine how much Maria and Sal would like to be here now, but I actually don't know. Perhaps they are here. I can't say if that were possible or even if that is the way of things. Maybe so many Souls or past people or Others are also in the room, and no one knows they aren't alone with Mike. That would be one crowded room. Sometimes, I wonder if my role is as special as I think. What am I thinking? I am the cord, for Source's sake!

If passed Maria, Sal, and Gloria were here, it would be a party with all these memories. Ahh, Maria. Maria was a pip. Albeit a bit of a saint-martyr, she carried the burden of all. Her cross to bear was very heavy, but I imagine that came from being an only child and primary caregiver for her folks, and also from just being a very good person. Maria had very high standards and expectations and exacted really solid and swift revenge. Maria had rules that only she could break.

Let's go back to 1978. The number one song on the radio was "Shadow Dancing" by Andy Gibb. Shrill and breathy. Cute, but not my thing. Mikey and Gloria were in the car with Maria, and they were going to see one of the Aunt Roses...the patent leather purse one.

Maria said, "Aunt Rose. She has cancer, and I'm just warning you, she has it bad now. I've been going every day to cook and clean for her and her family, but I want you to see her now before we regret it. Now, I want to warn you that she has a bit of a cancer smell. Aunt Rose is very conscious of it, and she does everything she can to cover the smell. This is part of life, and you just have to get used to it. You do things in life you do not enjoy, but you do hard things for people, especially family. So…if either of you says anything about the cancer smell, I will kill you. Do you understand? You will not live to see another day. I will smack you so hard in the head, you will forget every episode of *The Brady Bunch*. You will die. Okay?"

Mike and Gloria screamed at the same time, "Okay!"

Maria yelled to the back seat of the car. "Let's go see Aunt Rose."

They walked in the door.

Maria flew into action, saying, "Aunt Rose! How are you today? How's your cancer smell? Shall I make meatloaf or soup?"

Gloria and Mike just looked at each other. What just happened? There are no rules.

That's the lesson. There are no rules with family.

CHAPTER 26

Hunchback was significant for many reasons. It was a fantastic show, probably one of the best-ever created for a theme park, beloved by guests and casts alike. It was 1 million degrees on stage, and it launched a new career for Mike.

Mike thought he'd stay for the eight-week rehearsal period, open the show, get the accolades, and then leave. That was the plan. But he fell in love with the show, the resources at hand for these kinds of shows, and found a fascination in the Park of Theme. He also sensed an opportunity. In his short time there, it seemed to Mike that there weren't many directors from the New York Theater scene, and he also sensed that the Famous Theme Park Company might be moving into more theatrical endeavors.

Many of their talented directors seemed to not have a NYC background. Again...this was from Mike's immediate circle of people he knew. He didn't know for sure, but he did have a feeling there were not a lot of directors who had worked in New York in the profession as directors. Mike thought he could bring something extra to the creative table.

Oh, yeah, Mike forgot about Brian again, too. Mike said he saw some long-term opportunity down in Florida and asked Brian if he would consider moving down for a new kind of life. Mike expected to hear Brian say, "Hell, no. Are you crazy? Florida blows."

Surprisingly, Brian said yes, and he got a job as an art director for an Orlando-based publishing company. It was amazing. Brian was happier than Mike was about the whole thing. Brian and Mike made friends. Life was good. They were making a living. They bought a house, and Mike and Brian broke up the first month they were in the house. However, they did stay as roommates and adored each other.

Then, opportunity knocked. Mike noticed nobody did any kind of cabaret-style work in Orlando. So much talent there, and no one did anything downtown that was racy and "so not theme park." So, Mike put on an annual cabaret with other fantastic park performers who were also friends. This annual cabaret caught the attention of some of the "creatives" at the theme park. They asked Mike if he'd like to be a Show Director for a holiday offering because his cabaret was so funny.

Mike asked, "What does 'Show Director' mean?"

The person said, "Well, they direct shows."

Mike tried to explain that being called a director implies that you do, indeed, direct a show, but this fell on deaf ears, and this theme park language was more difficult than Cantonese. Just for the record, go try calling Jerry Zaks a Show Director and see what he says.

Mike said okay; he'd be a Show Director, which is redundant as far as he was concerned, and that was done. Mike's holiday show was a hit, and on New Year's Eve, 1998, Mike was asked by a high-level producer what else he'd like to do in the parks. Mike said he wanted to re-do the out of order, not quite story driven, and more of a revue-styled version of the *Beauty and Beast* show that had been running in one of the parks.

Mike loved the *Beauty and the Beast* show, but he saw an incredible opportunity to make it even better. The current show had been running in the park for quite a while. The cast was fantastic, jam-packed with excellent singers and dancers, but these amazing performers were not asked to use their full potential. Plus, in Mike's humble opinion, the show was missing the very heart of the story. The show is about loving something you would never consider loving before because of the strength and clarity-giving power of true love. That thematic piece was missing. Those lines in those scenes that make those moments were missing. The details were not there.

Mike considered *Beauty and the Beast* to be the crown jewel of the animation industry. The film had an Oscar nomination, for God's sake. In fact, after seeing the animated classic *Beauty and the Beast* in New York,

Mike actually thought there might be a place for him at the Famous Theme Park Company. That's how moved Mike was by this beautiful film. With all that, Mike thought the park was presenting an abstracted view and essence of this timeless tale. The producer asked what it would take for Mike to accomplish his vision for a reimagined *Beauty and the Beast*.

Mike said, "One cast, one room, one music director, and leave me alone."

One week later, the show was done and ready for review and to be approved by the creatives. The show was a rave; it was remounted, and it ran for a very long time. That was one of Mike's favorite projects of all time. And thus, Mike's long successful career as a Show Director began.

Famous Theme Park Company is a global company, and some new creatives were hired in California. Mike ended up working extensively with these new creative leaders in the Glendale offices. Mike liked all of them, save one self-absorbed and incompetent leader. And she got fired...so wee! The new team in California turned out to be, over the years, very smart and collaborative.

Work continued, and Mike became known as the "kick ass and take names" director. So many shows, press events, large-scale spectaculars, and intimate street shows. Mike was in another renaissance of his career. And then something completely unexpected happened; something a psychic told him would happen 15 years earlier. And Mike had the cassette tape recording to prove it.

CHAPTER 27

The year was 1983, and Mike went to a psychic convention at the War Memorial Convention Center in Rochester, New York. The place was booth after booth, line after line, filled with psychics. Amazing. Mike went with his friend, Wendy, who was really into this kind of thing. Readings were usually around $15, and you got a cassette recording of the session. Mike wandered around the convention center, searching. He wanted a reading from someone who felt *just right*...or Dionne Warwick, who was nowhere to be found.

Mike sensed something. I know what you're thinking, and no, it was not Angel #4. Mike sat down at the table of this large-ish man who had an "I had incense going, but the fire marshal made me snub it out an hour ago" smell. The man was a bit gruff and said, "Cards, Palm, Runes, hold your ring...what?"

Mike asked him if he could get a general impression without any of those things. The man gave a blank stare, so Mike said he didn't care. The large man pressed the record button on the tape recorder, stated his name, the date, and Mike's name. And then they were on an unbelievable roll.

Although the reading started quite mundane, it then got quite unique. It seemed Mike was going east. Not just east like Boston, but Far East. China, in fact. This move was to happen in a number of years. The man looked up like he had a gas bubble.

"Do you work with puppets?"

"Huh?"

"Do you work with puppets?"

"God. No. GOD, NO!"

"Well, I see you with puppets. Yes...there will be a large change in your life." The gruff man made a curious face and said, "Who is the little boy?"

Mike wasn't sure he heard the question correctly.

"Huh?"

"The little boy. You've seen him, right?"

Mike was very clear with his next sentence: "No...no, I have not."

"He's standing right next to you."

Mike looked to one side then the other. He didn't see the little boy.

"You're not going to see him now if you haven't seen him yet. He's with you all the time."

Mike didn't know what to say, so he relied on being funny.

"Does he vacuum? Because I hate vacuuming." Though he wouldn't admit it, Mike was chilled to the bone.

Wendy walked into Mike's reading booth and said, "Hi!"

Mike said, "Wendy, don't stand there; you may or may not be standing on a little boy."

The gruff man looked annoyed, more by the fact they were interrupted than by Mike's snarky comment.

"Who's this?"

"My friend, Wendy."

"Should she stay?"

"I think so...let me bring her up to speed. I'm going to China with puppets and, apparently, I have a little boy with me all the time. How did your reading go?"

Wendy said she paid a lady $15 for the sea witch to tell her that she would never marry.

I could have told her that for $10. But money means nothing to me. I'm just a Soul.

Wendy went on, "Let's hear more about the little boy."

The gruff man closed his eyes.

"Do you know any children who died young in your family? This child is a relative."

Mike said, "Not that I can think of. Unless you mean my little cousin who died under suspicious circumstances while Whiskey Jenny was taking him on the subway and he fell onto the tracks. Personally, I feel she pushed him... Do you mean him?"

The man waited. He took a long deep breath in and then exhaled.

"Nope. Not him. He says his name is Charlie."

"So, I have a little boy named Charlie with me all the time. Why?"

The man extended his hand to touch Mike's hand.

"He is looking out for you."

"Does Charlie by any chance have puppets, because I really hate puppets."

"He doesn't have puppets."

"Is he Chinese?"

"Do you have any Chinese relatives?"

"No."

"Then how can he be Chinese?"

This began to feel a bit like an interrogation.

The gruff man put on his business face.

"Look, Mike... It's Mike, right? You have five minutes left in your session and two minutes left with my patience. As a recap, in the future, you're going Far East, you will have something to do with puppets, and you have a child with you named Charlie."

"Is Charlie an Angel?'

"Not that I know of. But he is a spirit, and he is with you all the time."

"Oh, my God, I can never pee again and feel comfortable when someone is watching."

The gruff man looked surprised.

"That's what you're worried about after all I told you?"

"I can be very pee shy."

Mike remembered they were still recording. So, Mike leaned into the recorder and said, "Not all the time, pee shy. Just occasionally. It's not an obsession or anything weird."

The gruff man was clearly done.

"Time's up. I hope you are satisfied with your reading."

"Satisfied? I'm terrified."

Wendy and Mike both left the booth.

Wendy seemed sullen and said, "And I'm never going to get married."

Mike felt her pain.

"God, we're a mess. I want a coffee."

"Me, too."

Mike looked to his left and said, "Charlie, go get us two coffees."

CHAPTER 28

Several years and shows later, the Famous Theme Park was opening a new park in Hong Kong. Mike went to China to bring the Park's brand to Asia. Essentially, Mike became an unofficial ambassador of Famous Theme Park to all of Asia, except Japan, which already had a theme park. This was a massive job. Creating shows for India to Australia was under the creative direction of Mike and a small but mighty team. Shows were created in Hindi, Vietnamese, Korean, Singaporean, Mandarin, Cantonese, and Shanghainese. It was an amazing life experience.

Mike had pictures of himself and two very famous mice mascots on top of the Sydney Opera House, the Great Wall of China, in the Taj Mahal, in Cambodia, Vanuatu, Pine Island, Tibet, Pakistan, and Cleveland, Ohio.

One of my favorite memories of this time was when Mike was to bring two famous mice to Vietnam for the first time since—well, maybe ever. Their communist government, beginning to open to business with the Famous Brand, asked for the two mice to make a grand appearance in Vietnam. So, Mike arrived with the two mascots in Vietnam, and they were immediately whisked to the old American Embassy that was taken by siege during the final hours of the Vietnam War. By the way, the Vietnam War has been stricken from all Vietnamese history books and banned from being talked about—ever—with a death sentence attached.

The military escort said this Vietnam Embassy was the perfect venue for the grand reveal of the rodents. He actually said "rodents." Now, there they were, just Mike and two mice from China. He found himself in the position to become a diplomat.

Mike said casually, "This venue, huh? Well, this is very difficult for us. Your Embassy was, at one time, our United States Embassy and, I don't know if you heard, but we had a mess of problem here that generated a whole Broadway musical." Mike pivoted. He thought of a better approach. "You see, thousands will come to see the mice, and this venue will only accommodate a few hundred people. Perhaps this venue would make the people unhappy that everyone could not see the rodents—I mean, mice."

There were about two minutes of very fast talking in Vietnamese. Then one military escort said, "Ah, we now understand. Yes, we understand your point. Do you have a venue in mind?"

Mike had never been to Vietnam. Then Mike had a thought.

"Do you have an arts center? Or a grand opera house?"

The escort said, "How about the Grand Opera House?"

"Yes! Good idea! I wish I thought of The Grand Opera House that I just mentioned two seconds ago. Let's go see that."

The Grand Opera House was perfect. It was at the very end of what seemed to be the main artery street of Ho Chi Minh City. It was gorgeous and had a balcony on the third floor where they could reveal the mice, and hundreds of thousands of people could see them for miles. The press! The publicity! This was a perfect compromise.

Very early the next morning, Mike rehearsed the rodents. Mike said to them, "Stay behind this curtain. Then we will play a magical theme song, newly recorded in Vietnamese, then you will be revealed, and hold for photos until I say stop, and we will draw the curtains again."

This was going to be perfect. They went to breakfast.

Mike noticed that crowds began to form on the street. This main street was completely shut down and lined with machine-gun-armed military. The escort said that a special invitation almost mandates this event by the Vietnamese Premier. It is his personal invitation. Everyone who could come, should come to this exciting Vietnamese event. Mike thought that was cool.

Following breakfast, Mike and the entourage returned to the Grand Opera House. Mike screeched, "Holy Mother of Pearl!"

While they were eating breakfast, the Communist Government had hung giant banners of Ho Chi Minh on either side of the balcony, three stories long and crazy wide. Mike collected himself and said, "Escort Person?"

"Yes, Mr. Mike."

Mike pointed toward the banners of Ho Chi Minh.

"Ummm...is that..."

"Xin Chao" (Sing Chow).

Mike misunderstood. He tried again.

"Hello...is that...?"

"Xin Chao."

Now a little annoyed, he replied again, "Hello. Good morning."

Asian languages can be very complex. Mike thought he kept saying hello, but he was saying yes to his unfinished question.

"So, that's Ho Chi Minh?"

"Xin Chao."

Mike became very animated.

"No Sing Chow!"

Mike raced into the room. By this time, there were thousands gathered in the street, but Mike did not care. The company had rules. The mice have rarely appeared with a seated United States President. They could certainly not appear standing book-ended by the man who caused one of the most controversial wars in the history of the United States where this very Famous Theme Park is based.

Mike burst through the curtains and onto the balcony. He went to the left side first and began pulling down the Ho Chi Minh banner. Gasps from the thousands below began. Mike thought to himself, *This is not happening...* and then he felt what seemed to be a cold metal object against his left temple.

"Mr. Mike. Perhaps you step away and come inside."

Mike simply said, "Sing Chow." Once inside, Mike was pushed into a red velvet chair that was actually very pretty. What wasn't so pretty were the four guards with machine guns pointed to Mike's head. *Okay...* he thought. This was a magical theme park job, right? Not Benghazi or something the Secretary of State would have to deal with. The guns were very close to Mike's head, yet Mike wasn't afraid. I mean, he grew up pulling heads off chickens.

This is when Mike got pissed. He stood up and flailed his arms like a jacked-up ballerina and said, "Don't point those guns at me. I saw *Miss Saigon* on Broadway three times, and I know how this ends." Needless to say, the military police did not know what to do. They looked confused. One looked like he had seen *Miss Saigon*, and Mike noticed he had the best-polished shoes. Okay...maybe he had one ally in this madness.

The door swung open, and everyone went to a snapped salute. A woman walked in. She was amazing. She acted with so much authority that even Mike wanted to salute. She rattled off something in Vietnamese. The guards went to one side of the room. She walked over to Mike, looking stunning, like a Vietnamese Julia Roberts at the Academy Awards.

She spoke.

"Mr. Mike."

"Yes."

"We have a problem."

"Yes, Sing Chow, we sure do!"

"Mr. Mike. The rodents will appear, or you will disappoint all the People of Vietnam and our ruler, and you will be placed in prison. And you desecrate Ho Chi Minh." Mike was really impressed she got out the word desecrate. That's a hard word.

Mike said that he understood, but that the mice would not appear alongside any political images. That was clearly stated in a contract. A contract that the Vietnamese government cannot change at will.

Ooo...she was sharp. But she wasn't as sharp as a gay American in Vietnam.

Mike flipped his switch and said, "Look, sis," as he pulled ever so slightly back the curtain. "How many people do you think are out there to see the rodents...I mean mice...by 'personal invitation' from your Premier? I mean, you said it yourself; it's on every flyer in the city and in every newspaper."

'Sis' said, "Tens of thousands." Oddly, she had trouble with the word "thousands."

"Yes. A lot. Maybe a million."

"Yes, we will not disappoint them, so the rodents will appear."

Mike snapped back with, "Not with those banners up."

She said, "Then they will not appear."

Mike said, "Fine with me. You just said it. C'mon, rodents—I mean, mice. Let's go. Just one more thing. When the rodents known as mice do not appear for the almost million people out there, who will the People of Vietnam blame? Probably not me. They don't know me. Not the rodents known as mice either; they love the rodents known as mice. Oh...yes. It will be the Premier; and he will blame you. And almost a million people will leave feeling that the United One People's Communist Government cannot even deliver rodents known as mice on a balcony. Now, get outta my way. I have a rather horrible van waiting to take us back to your awful airport to get us on a plane from 1972 to take us back to Hong Kong."

Mike took two steps away. He heard her behind him.

"Stop."

Mike abruptly turned to her like Cameron Diaz with a dash of Drew Barrymore mixed in and said, "Yes?"

He heard a bunch of Vietnamese.

The military guards went out to the balcony and returned in seconds carrying two unfolded and yanked-down banners of Ho Chi Minh.

The elegant woman said, "The rodents will go on, yes?"

Mike, like Meryl Streep accepting another Academy Award, said, "Sing Chow."

CHAPTER 29

Wendy walks into Mike's room.

"Wendy," I want to say, but can't, of course. She is still alive... duh. Wendy goes over to Mike's bedside and says, "It was quite a ride, wasn't it, Mike?" Wendy doesn't look so great herself, but hey, she is in her late eighties, too. "I will miss you. But I know we will see each other again."

She is right! I like this.

A man walks into the room.

"Hon?"

"One more minute, Mark."

Wendy had gotten married! Wow. Her psychic sucked.

Mark says that the nurse said they could only stay a minute or two.

"Alright." Putting her hand on his, she says, "Mike, you were my best friend."

Mark says, "I thought I was your best friend."

"You're my husband, Mark." Seeing the look on his face, she says, "Okay, yes, but this is different."

Mark goes over to her, and they walk out of the room together. Mark goes through the doorway first. Wendy stops...

And turns...

And says...

"Oh! Hello, Charlie, wherever you are in this room. You'll be able to leave him soon."

I wonder why I can't see Charlie. Even now, so close to the end. The Source is so elusive and mystifying. But then again, who would want the ultimate life source to be mundane and predictable, right?

I can feel the cord tighten. Three hours left. Maximum. I really enjoyed being Mike's Soul. But I've been a soul for a few other real pips through the eons.

Top of the list, Madame Marie Curie. What the hell was she thinking, holding all that uranium all the time? My God, what a whack job. Do you know what her last words were?

"They're gone. My hands."

And I said, "Oui, Marie."

No disrespect. She was a genius and changed history, but holding uranium in your hands? C'mon.

Then there's Mr. Campbell Selt. Not really famous. Not particularly remarkable, but definitely interested in other people. Campbell was born in Kansas City, Missouri, in 1888. The number one song on the radio was nothing. You had to wait until 1895 for that invention. Campbell was the son of Judith and Wilmont Selt, mercantile store owners. They lived in a traditional Victorian house, and life went on as it typically did back then... until Campbell moved out on his own at 18 to raise corn in fields he bought with his savings from working at the store. Still pretty boring, I know. I lived it.

One night, Campbell was out drinking at the local pub and met a man who turned out to be his best friend, Bill Dubilier. You might say that Bill was a journeyman, lived in Alaska for a stint, and fancied himself an inventor of sorts. This fascinated Campbell, and they talked for hours. Bill was fascinated by the work being done with electronic waves by inventors worldwide, like Marconi, Popov, and Fessenden. Bill knew there was a breakthrough right around the corner somewhere, and he was going to be the one to figure it out. Bill explained that you could take sound and run it up an antenna, and those audible sounds would turn into waves that travel at the speed of sound. But how to hear them once they were gone out into the air?

Campbell thought for a minute and said, "It's like corn."

"What?"

"A corn harvest. You harvest it up in the air, but if nothing is catching the corn, the corn just goes back to the ground. That's why you put a wagon behind the tractor. You catch the ears of corn thrown up in the air. Just put up another antenna and see if it catches the waves and turns the waves back into audible sound."

On December 24, 1906, Bill and Campbell (along with many genius predecessors) had what was considered the first radio broadcast. And the number one song, and only song, on the radio, was "Oh, Holy Night."

Yup, he was a good one to Soul with.

CHAPTER 30

Once Hong Kong Famous Theme Park was built, Mike became the Creative Director for that park and Asia. And life was never routine. You thought Americans had holidays? The Chinese have all those holidays, plus dozens more. Chinese New Year alone was two full weeks of events, tradition, and leisure.

With a rich history of well over 5,000 years, China and its people taught Mike many things that were beyond his mere 40 years on Earth. China changed Mike for the better. His eyes were opened wider than ever before. He learned a higher level of respect for people's unique cultures. Mike had new inspiration to learn more, an appreciation for a different way of selfless thinking. Mike learned that "I" is less important than "us."

Mike also depended on his Chinese colleagues who helped him in every way to navigate his life in China. From simply paying a utility bill to the procedures of meetings with ranks of respect, his Chinese colleagues had his back. Mike would have been lost without the care and gentle handling by his Chinese friends.

Because the Chinese have so many days or weeks to be celebrated, Mike learned to do many events at the same time, working at warp speed. Whether it was a new building opening day tradition or Chinese New Year, each event had to be new and inventive. Asia moves at the speed of light, and if you are not the first with an idea or concept, you are not even last. You are nothing.

Mike was everywhere all the time and became known as the Mayor of the Mid-levels. Hong Kong is built on giant and exceptionally steep mountains. Then these high-rises 100 stories or more are built on them. It's like a disaster waiting to happen. Between these high-rises are narrow streets. There's the coast level, the mid-level, and the peaks. Like Victoria's Peak, the best view of Hong Kong with the most antiquated cable car ride up to the top. Mike lived in the mid-levels and literally went to every restaurant and ate there at one time or another. Everyone knew Mike, and he rarely even had to pay for a meal. Now, this wasn't a freebie. Mike recommended restaurants to many colleagues, and all they had to say was, "Mike sent us."

Life was good, but it was not easy. English was not as prevalent as the Ex-Pats began leaving Hong Kong. English was no longer taught in school, so it was mainly the older Chinese who could converse in English. Mike found it difficult to communicate in one language, English, but had to remind himself his Chinese colleagues usually knew three to four other languages, including English.

Mike was based in Hong Kong, but his travels took him to Thailand, and he learned about the many Buddhas and what they all meant. He spent four months in India for work and saw such despair and illness. So much. Slums that go on forever. He saw children washing in filthy street water. He also saw beautiful people with happiness as their true essence. He also saw a camel walk by his hotel window with a monkey on his back. The monkey waved to Mike.

Mike knew it was time to leave Hong Kong and relocate back to the United States when he had a nervous breakdown asking for an envelope from the front desk clerk in his apartment building. Mike could not learn Cantonese. No one can unless you live there for like 10 years. I don't know how to describe it, except there seem to be only six words, each with 19 tones of how to say the word. Mike's breakdown happened when he wanted an envelope. Phonetically, envelope in Cantonese is "seun fung." But if you use different tones, you could be saying "east," "clam," "baby carriage," "Elvis Presley"...you get the idea. Now, Mike had successfully said seun fung many times before and did, in fact, get an envelope. That was not happening that day.

Not receiving an envelope, Mike kept getting louder and louder, now screaming, "SEUN FUNG... SEUN FUNG ... SEUN FUNG!" Then he resorted to acting out writing a letter and sticking it in an envelope and licking the glue, all while screaming, "SEUN FUNG!"

Finally, the receptionist said, "Ah! Seun fung," and he gave Mike the envelope. Mike said thank you, and as he walked away, he heard the receptionist guy say, "You coulda just said envelope."

Mike was done. He got a transfer back to the United States just before Christmas in 2010. The number one song was playing on the radio as his plane left the Chinese ground. It was "Private Corner" by Jacky Cheung, Mike's good friend.

CHAPTER 31

Charlie. The boy that the psychic guy told Mike about was supposed to be a relative. Soon after his psychic reading, Mike called his mom and asked who the little boy was. Was it that boy who Aunt Jenny killed by throwing him in the subway because she was crazy?

I think that kid's name was Gio, and it wasn't proven that she threw him into the subway tracks, although she was never quite the same after that subway trip. Thus, the nickname "Whiskey Jenny." Mike also asked many other family members if anyone named Charlie died at a young age.

One of Mike's Aunt Roses said that her brother, Charlie, died very young. Mike was excited! Wow, maybe that was Charlie!

"How old was he?"

"45."

Okay...not that Charlie.

Then, one casual night at dinner, Gramma Rose mentioned that she had a twin brother no one ever really talked about.

Maria said, "What?"

"Well, we didn't really talk about tuberculosis then, and I had it myself and was sent to Arizona for a year when I was four to help with the healing. But Charlie, my twin, died."

Bingo...Charlie. But why did Charlie want to hang around me? he wondered.

Mike explained the entire psychic experience to Gramma Rose, but she said that was ridiculous and that couldn't happen.

Mike said, "Well, why not, Gram?"

Gramma said, "Because Charlie didn't know you. He was dead like 50 years before you were born."

"Gram, that's not how it works."

Gramma said, with a very stoic voice, "Oh, please…tell me how it works."

"Gram, people die, and then the Supreme Being asks them to stay with you to help you."

"Like to get you coffee and vacuum your rugs?"

Again with the vacuuming. Why did this mundane housekeeping routine come up again? I guess people hate to vacuum.

"Gram, I have not seen Charlie vacuum. I think it's more of a being there for you in times of stress and turmoil thing."

Gramma thought for a moment.

"Why wouldn't Charlie pick me? I'm his sister. His twin sister."

"Well, Gram, I kinda thought you would find it fascinating and actually quite beautiful that Charlie has decided to stay with me as a guardian through my life."

"Mikey, I am happy for you, but I never liked Charlie."

"Why's that?"

"He was Pop's favorite. Not me."

"I'm sure you're wrong about that. What makes you think Pop liked Charlie better than you?"

"Well, one day, Pop sat me on his knee and held me close, laid my head on his chest, and said, 'I like Charlie better than you.'"

"Well, at least Pop wasn't vague."

Mike had to test this Charlie thing one more time. He went to a psychic community and chose another psychic. Yep. At the very end, she did say, "You know you have a little boy with you, right?"

Mike said, "Oh, you must mean Charlie."

"I didn't know his name, but he's here to help you."

Mike said, "He hasn't done anything for me that I could notice."

The psychic smiled ever so lightly.

"Of course. His job is to help you avoid things you never knew could have hurt you."

"Oh. Do you think you can ask him to vacuum?"

The psychic did not know if this was a joke or not. It was not.

"That will be $25 for the reading. Have you asked him? You know, to vacuum...to clean up a bit?"

"I can do that?"

"Yes! He's here for you."

"Cool! Charlie, will you vacuum for me?"

The psychic went into what looked like a fake trance.

Mike waited for an answer.

Mike looked at the psychic.

The psychic said, "Charlie said, 'What's a vacuum?'"

CHAPTER 32

The year was 2020. The number one song on the radio was "Toosie Slide" by Drake.

Mike was turning 59 years old, and this was a hard birthday for him. In his mind, 59 really meant 60, and a 60-year-old gay man who is not yet married just becomes an old Whiskey Aunt Jenny. Or Angelina. Or Aunt Nancy. Mike's parents had now been married for 64 years. This was mind-blowing and beautiful to Mike. Sure, they had hard times. Sure, they hated each other. Sure, they loved each other. But...they had each other.

Mike's whole life was in search of his life partner. He wanted this more than anything. But did he? He had plenty of relationship opportunities but always ended up putting his career first. And it worked...or so it seemed. He married his career, and now at 59, it wasn't enough.

What to do?

Nothing. Keep living. Keep being yourself.

Maybe Mike was not meant to marry. I didn't know because we were living the same life.

Mike wanted to be a Broadway star, then switched to being a Creative Director for the world's largest and most prolific entertainment company in the world. Mike had won awards, directed film, television, sports, and Broadway stars, and he became a Famous Theme Park Legacy. It even came with a nametag and a statue. All this would be a dream for hundreds of people. But you can't hug an award statue at night. I mean...you can kiss it, but it's not very satisfying. There's a metal after taste. Don't ask.

Some would wonder if Mike would have done things differently, but I know that Mike had no choice. This was his path. I saw his life choice at the very beginning of it all, and I chose to go along. What did this all mean? I decided that Mike's life was perfect just the way it was, and I hope that Mike thought it was perfect, too.

CHAPTER 33

Let's review Mike's boyfriends.

Firstly, there's Stuart. He wasn't technically a boyfriend, but he was the man who took Mike's virginity. Stuart was the musical director of *Bye Bye Birdie*. Of course, nothing for Mike could be normal. So, that very afternoon, after the "cherry popping," Mike hopped in a taxi, and the first thing he heard in that taxi ride from Queens back to Manhattan is, "Gay men are dying because of gay sex, and it is believed the virus began with cats." Not the Broadway show, but felines. The Broadway show *Cats* can cause other medical problems. Boredom, malaise, lethargy, vomiting, and in the worst cases, suicide.

Mike thought this was God's grand warning, and it ruined sex for Mike for the rest of his life... Well... At least for a couple of years. However, it did instill an irrational fear about blood, seeing blood, sex, spit, tears, sweat...basically anything. This was really traumatic for Mike. And, on top of hearing the traumatic news about a new virus named AIDS, Mike had to go to his Manhattan College Senior Prom that night with Mary Ann O'Brian. Mike's head began to spin.

I have AIDS, and I have to wear a beige tux... Why did I choose beige? And why am I going to the senior prom with Mary Ann O'Brian?

It had nothing to do with Mary Ann. She was amazing and one of the best actresses Mike had ever seen. She had asked him to go to prom. He was blown away and honored. But at this moment in the taxi, all he could think was, *Why? Why tonight, the day I got AIDS, and now I'll have to think about THAT all night.*

The night was ruined for him. He wondered how he would ever know if he was well.

There was so little information about AIDS back then. For Pete's sake, people! Medical professionals were saying the virus jumped from cats! Jumped from cats? How does a disease jump from a cat? Was it like fleas? Do fleas have sex? Do they have AIDS? And it was his very first time. This was just too much to understand. Mike was lucky he never got it, but over the years, he met many people who had become infected on their first time. They just didn't know enough about it back then.

Mike got out of the taxi and decided to take a nap. He would push the whole thing away for a while, get dressed, and go to the prom. Mike's head hurt. Suppression was so taxing. Mary Ann, in a very pretty dress and heels, walked into the prom with Mike. The song the DJ was playing was Dolly Parton's "9 to 5." Well, there you go. Things weren't going to be so bad after all.

Okay, back to Mike's boyfriends. Next was John. John's best attribute was that he smoked well. Mike thought he looked good smoking. That was that.

Then there was Walter, a famous architect now, but who wore way too much cologne. I mean an overwhelming amount of Calvin Klein's original scent. He was gorgeous but so aromatic that it wasn't romantic.

Then came Nick, a narcissist who still owes Mike $10,000. And that's without the interest.

And Brian, who was perfect and Mike's biggest mistake. As I said, Mike chose career over love.

CHAPTER 34

The year was 2035, and it was New Year's Eve. If you're keeping track, Mike was now 74 years old. He never thought he would actually ever get that old. Mike used to talk to his friends, Andy, Donna, Patty, and Brian, about how old 50 was going to feel, how in the future they would someday actually be 50. It was outrageous to think that Mike was now 74, and he made no bones about it. He did not like talking about it. There was not enough moisturizer in the world to smooth out 74. He was at his wit's end, too, about the prospect of ever or never finding the love of his life.

That was about to change.

Jim Franklin was a retired lawyer from the Upper West Side vacationing in a Florida condo complex he had bought for himself. The complex was called The Grove Lakes. What the hell did that mean? Were there trees in a lake? The state of Florida has a terrible reputation for naming housing developments. They all sounded the same...Wintermere, Windermere, Winter Garden, Winter Park, The Shanties of Foreclosureton.

Anyway, Mike was retired then, too, and lived at The Grove Lakes full-time. Jim and Mike met at the pool. Just two leathered-skinned old coots who got a kick out of each other. They talked with ease about the many things they had in common. They had New York in common, for one. Mike loved to talk about the law. Jim loved to talk about show business. They ended up being a wonderful couple, and Jim sold his loft in Manhattan, and together they bought the top-of-the-line condominium The Grove Lakes had to offer: The Frontier Suite.

Yes, The Frontier Suite with the wild frontier view of the Walmart across from the Golden Corral, just down the street from the JoAnn Fabrics and, luckily, near to the Michaels for all the crafts Jim and Mike loved to do—which was none. Mike and Jim did have excellent taste, and that condo looked amazing. They were happy. Mike was happy. I had never really seen Mike happy before. Mike had amazing friends, an amazing career, amazing journeys; but always a deep loneliness with a dash of sadness, too. Although happy together, Mike and Jim were not in love. They were just great companions with love for each other.

They had five fun years together, and then Jim died of a heart attack. Mike was by his side and as stable as anyone could be. Years of being alone, maybe being held at gunpoint in Vietnam…who knows what made Mike strong. Mike was sad. But Mike would go on. After all, it was slated that Mike would die at 89 in the year 2050. It was to be so, and there would be no change to that.

CHAPTER 35

As you can imagine, Mike's upbringing was not only very Italian but very Catholic. Let's take a visit to Mike when he went to confession at the Vatican in Vatican City, Italy. Talk about an unexpected visit. Mike was in Rome working on a new project for Famous Theme Park with Famous Cruise Ships. A third-party dance and technology company combined dance, acrobatics, photosensitive light, and a canvas for a remarkable experience. This group did, however, need a helping hand from a theme park specialist. Hence, Mike's involvement.

While in Rome, Mike had his fiftieth birthday and decided to go to the Vatican to see what all the fuss and wealth was about. He waited in line for literally four hours to get into the Vatican. Holy Moly, that place was amazing. It was gorgeous. It was a sensory overload of gold. It was magnificent, and to Mike, it felt holy, too. He did not expect that he would feel humbled and like he was in the presence of God. He also did not know God had so much gold. Only Aunt Connie had almost as much gold, and most of that was yellowed and low quality.

There was this roped-off area with a very subtle sign that read *Confessions*. Mike thought, *Why not?* He walked up, and there was no line. That was odd. This was Italy. The Catholic epicenter of being Catholic. With much adultery. A Swiss Military Guard asked if Mike was Catholic. Mike said yes. Apparently, only Catholics can confess at the Vatican.

Now, back at home at Our Lady of Tears... Why is she always so sad? She's literally the only person who never died, but ascended. C'mon, that is cool and something to at least be happy about. Anyway, back to the church...you confessed in a small two-room booth. You knew to wait for the door to slide open, and there was a very hard-to-see through screen between you and the priest.

You would say, "Bless me, Father, for I have sinned. It has been six months from my last confession." The priest would ask what your sins were, and you'd make them up. You needed some that sounded routine and then you'd add one just to make the priest feel good about his job. The priest would give you a simple penance of a series of prayers—like five Hail Marys and an Act of Contrition—and then you could check that off your family's required monthly bucket list.

Nope. Not in Rome. You get past the Swiss Guards, and there are about 15 booths. Each booth has the language in which you would confess displayed. Mike chose English. There was no line, and he went into his side. The priest pushed back the wall, and *BAM*, there he was. No screen! What, are they nuts?

Mike screamed, and it was audible.

The priest said, "What's wrong?'

Mike said, "Where's the thing?

"The what?"

"The screen thing. Is it out for repair?"

"We don't have a screen thing. What are you talking about?"

"The screen thing. What kind of priest are you? You're not supposed to actually see me."

"Well, I'm the priest here, and I think I know what I'm doing."

"Well, at Our Lady of Tears in New York, where I'm from, when you go to confession, there's a separation between you and the priest with a screen. A screen. With all that gold out there, you can't find enough money for a screen?"

"Why should there be a separation between you and a priest?"

"I'm just a little shocked to see you, that's all."

The priest tried to bring the confession back on track.

"You are Catholic, right?"

"Of course! You think I could fool a Swiss Guard?"

"Okay. Let's begin."

Mike said, "Bless me, Father, for..."

The priest interrupted. "We don't do that here."

"Huh?"

"You are an American, no?"

"No. I mean, yes. I mean, I am an American Catholic. I was even an altar boy."

"That's good."

"No, Father, it was not."

"Why is that?"

"Well, you know how you ring the bells when the priest says certain things during the mass?"

"Yes. I am a priest at the Vatican. I could pontificate on for years about bells."

"Of course. Well, I thought whenever the priest was a little boring, I would add bells. You know, just to jazz it up a bit."

"You thought you'd jazz up a ceremony that has taken place for thousands of years?"

"I'm in show business."

"Ah...makes sense. Okay, it that your sin?"

"No."

"We just tell what you are sorry for. What is your name?"

"Mike."

"Michael. What are you sorry for?"

"I'm sorry there's no screen."

The priest laughed.

"Okay, please confess your sins."

"Well, it's my birthday..."

"That's not a sin.'

"I know, but I thought it would be amazing to confess my sins in the Vatican and then call my mother, and she would think this was the most special day of her life."

"Why would this not be your most special day in your life?"

"Well, Father, I don't really think I've sinned so big. A little jealously here, a little greed. But sins...do I need a man to forgive me?"

"Yes."

"Oh."

"Yes, you do, Michael, because you are telling a man who is objective and who can relieve you of what burdens you carry, and then you can feel forgiven by God, because God forgives you."

Mike just had to say it.

"I don't agree."

"What?"

"I just don't agree."

"Maybe that's your sin, Michael. Not that you disagree with the teachings of God's church, but you are blind to what you may be sinning about." Again, with the blind!

"No. Like, Father, I'm gay. The church used to say that's a sin."

"We aren't fond of it, no." In response to that, all Mike could think was, *Really…you aren't?* But he chose to keep that on the inside as he could smell that this conversation was going somewhere fun.

Mike said, "But something is either wrong or right, and if you as the Church cannot even decide what is the ultimate wrong and right, why do you feel that you can forgive anyone?"

The priest elbowed the Filipino priest in the booth right next to our English confessional and said, "I got a talker here."

The Filipino priest said, "A talker, I'll be right in."

In moments, the Filipino priest was in the booth with the English-speaking priest. Yup, side by side.

"Father Ronnie, this is Michael. Michael, this is Father Ronnie from Ta Al."

Mike got excited.

"Hey… I've been there!"

Father Ronnie said, "Did you climb the volcano?"

"Of course, I mean, why else would you go to Ta Al?"

"Yes, that's true. Father Enzio, have you been to Ta Al?"

The English-speaking priest must have been named Father Enzio.

"No, I haven't."

Mike said, "Well that's a sin. It's beautiful. Oh…wait…not a real sin."

"I know what you meant."

Father Ronnie continued, speaking much like a tour guide.

"Enzio, we should go. You'd like it. We can have lunch on the side of the volcano."

Father Enzio said, "It sounds lovely, but that's not why we are here."

Father Ronnie checked himself and said, "Oh, yes, we have…uh…we have with us today…"

Mike said, "Mike."

Father Enzio, "Michael. Yes."

Father Ronnie asked, "Why is Michael here?"

Father Enzio said, "Michael thinks this is all nonsense."

Father Ronnie seemed agitated. "No! Ta Al is a volcano, and you can have lunch on the side of the volcano. It's not nonsense."

Now, even Mike thought this was getting odd.

Father Enzio said, "Ronnie. This is about Michael's confession. Not about a volcano and lunch. Shall we begin? Michael came in today because it is his birthday, and he thought it would be lovely to make a confession at the Vatican and then call his mother."

"Oh! That's nice! Happy Birthday!"

Father Enzio struggled to continue with, "Yes, very nice, but Michael has something inside him that he needs to tell us, and he does want recognition and forgiveness of that feeling inside of him."

Mike was a bit confused.

"I do?"

"You do."

Father Ronnie said, "What is it, Michael? "

Mike cleared his throat and began. "Well…I think that it doesn't matter that Jesus rose from the dead, but he did so much good on Earth that the only way the people could recount this for ages was to say, 'Jesus rose from the dead to save us all.' And what they really meant was that he lived a pure and good life here on Earth."

The Filipino priest, Ronnie, said, "I better go get Angelo."

Okay…Mike had been in this confessional now about 20 minutes for something thing that usually takes five minutes or less. Plus, it was almost 5:00 P.M., and the Vatican closes at 5:00 P.M.

Father Ronnie came back with Father Angelo and another priest named Yugo, from Serbia. Yugo had to join Mike's side of the booth because Father Enzio's side was now jam-packed with three priests.

"Hello. I'm Father Yugo. The Serbia confession side was very slow today, and Ronnie said that there was some good dialogue going on here."

"Hi. I'm Michael. Mike."

Father Enzio recounted Mike's theory that it didn't matter that Jesus rose from the dead.

Yugo said, "Well, the story is better if he rises from the dead, Michael."

Mike was surprised.

"Story? What is this, a screenplay? Guys, my parents have dedicated their lives to going to church almost every day to pray for everyone, but mostly me and Gloria."

Father Yugo asked, "Who is Gloria?"

Father Enzio said, "Yugo, it does not matter who Gloria is."

Father Angelo said, "I'd like to know who Gloria is. It helps the story. You know, for the details."

Father Ronnie said, "Yes, I agree. See, Enzio? It will be better if we know who Gloria is."

Mike decided to bring the conversation about Gloria to a close and said, "Gloria is my sister."

Father Yugo said, "Oh, that is such a nice name."

Father Ronnie added, "Like in Excelsis Deo. So nice."

Father Enzio slapped his hands to his knees, let out a big sigh, and said, "Okay. Good. We all know who Gloria is. Okay. We go on. Here's the deal. It doesn't matter what you believe, as long as you believe you are saved by Jesus Christ."

Mike said, "What about God? Aren't you supposed to believe in God?"

Father Yugo said, "Around here, it's the same thing. Jesus and God. Same, same."

Father Anthony added, "Yes. Like the milk from the goat or the milk from the cow...she's the same milk."

Father Enzio said, "Thank you, Anthony, for that detailed analysis. But Michael, do you truly believe in God in your heart?"

Mike said that he did truly believe in God with all his heart.

Father Enzio said, "You are forgiven, Michael, and I...Father Ronnie, Father Anthony, and Father Yugo absolve you of your sins."

Mike hadn't recalled actually telling the priests any sins, but felt like this was a good way to end this conversation and, quite honestly, the confessional booth was beginning to feel like a clown car. Mission accomplished. Vatican seen. Absolved of sins. An unlikely birthday conversation with four priests. Not bad for a Friday.

Father Ronnie said, "We must go. Closing time."

Lovely chimes rang, and when the five of them emerged from the same booth, there was a definite quizzical look from the three Swiss Guards. The Vatican was nearly empty by then, and Mike walked out of there making small chit chat about this and that with four Catholic priests and three Swiss Army Guards. At the door, they all waved goodbye, and Father Enzio said, "Happy birthday, and now call your mother."

...and Mike did.

CHAPTER 36

Yup, we are up to the puppets. Remember the psychic? Remember the moving to China thing? He was right about all that, and now he was right about the puppets. Mike was named Artistic Director for a remake of an old show that sounded like "Travels of the Rather Small Fish Girl." This show was a black light puppet show, and you could say it was…dated. Mike learned how to manipulate puppets, make the puppets look like they had eye focus, look like they were speaking in real-time, and make them sing.

Mike had such respect for his many puppeteer mentors, and he learned to have a great appreciation for this art form where the puppeteer disappears, and the puppet comes to life. It was magical. The only downfall was that now Mike became 'the puppet guy' and was assigned to a show that sounded a lot like "A Large Hairy Animal You See in The Mountains and His Very Large Turquoise House." This show was amazing. The puppet interaction and the joy that these well-known puppets brought to the younger audience and their families was breathtaking.

Mike did have a problem though. The puppeteers were under the stage and had to move around underneath swiftly while changing between several puppets. It was a scramble under there, and the show became dangerous. The show closed for one week, and Mike went under that stage with a few collaborative experts and tried to figure it out.

Mike lived under that stage. The show operated with eight puppets and five puppeteers. There were four trap doors. There were arteries of metal support beams under there. And then it hit him. Literally, it hit him in the head. A metal beam as he was maneuvering and moving from downstage to upstage from playing a little titter of a mouse to playing a twin of another puppet.

If only Mike could have used that beam to propel himself to the next trap door and wheel himself swiftly over it.

Wheel! Wheel seat! Seat with wheels! Use the vast number of support beams to pull yourself and wheel about. Pull wheel. Go. See Mike. See Mike pull and go. Mike goes fast…

Why was Mike talking like a caveman reading a book for children? It could've been the hit to the head on the beam. But, let's blame the puppets.

Anyway…the wheel seat was the answer. That was it, and now to do a prototype. Mike, his fellow artists, and puppet masters took a round, wooden piece of plywood and attached rotating wheels under it. Mike was now able to propel around underneath the stage, using the arteries of beams and getting to the new trap door. Mike and the team choreographed each puppeteer route and changed the staged puppeteer patterns, and this really worked. Until they realized they had a problem: Different heights of the puppet and different heights of the performers. If only you could change the height of your seat.

Eureka! Different circular pads—well, pillows first for Mike—that could be added or taken away as the show went on, easily changing your height. This eventually evolved into very expensive seats with air compressors that made the circular seat go up and down, but this was the long version of how Mike got involved with puppets.

And that psychic knew all about it; and it is all preserved on Mike's cassette tape. Except Mike no longer had anything to play it back on. And, who would Mike play it for now in the year 2050, anyway? It's just a great memory.

CHAPTER 37

J ust like his mother, Maria, Mike invented rules to live by.

Before getting out of bed, pray about something.

Then, check your work email and answer the easily answered questions that came in during the night from a global company. This is just a bunch of work done quickly, and you can feel prepared for your day.

Then, while still in bed, stretch. This is key once you turn 40-ish. You can actually pull a muscle or throw your back out just getting out of bed after you start that fifth decade.

Pee and have a cup of coffee.

Enjoy a pretty view while having that cup of coffee. If there isn't a pretty view, buy or paint a picture you like.

Make your bed. Just do it. It makes everything seem all put together.

Brush your teeth, shave, and trim things that need trimming.

Then lay down, because, as an Italian man, shaving is exhausting.

Then shower, dress, and do that kind of thing.

Don't trust anyone who uses a crystal or stone as a deodorant.

When driving to work, think of everything you hate about your job or day ahead and then lose all those hateful thoughts and walk in the door and say hello to everyone.

Try to remember something about a colleague's life and ask them about it.

Get to work, be fast, and keep an open-door policy with everyone. Be accessible. Be creative. Inspire others by planting seeds, but not a fully gestated idea; they'll take it and claim it as their own. Visit people you don't usually see during your regular day. This will keep you fresh.

Have fun at work and keep things on track by being highly functioning and entertaining.

If someone is having trouble, talk to them, and you will help them, and you will learn something, too.

I know this all sounds like a "how to succeed" manual, but I'm not done.

Here's the "crazy" list of Mike's rules:

Never wear red and black together. You will always look like Belinda Carlisle.

Never hang wind chimes. Your neighbors hate wind chimes. Wind chimes are awful. Wind chimes are not calming. They clang and keep you up all night. Never hang wind chimes.

Stevie Nicks makes your ears bleed.

If you are throwing a party, always look better and more refreshed than your guests.

Prepare for the party way ahead and have it all set out one hour before the party and then lay down and rest.

Enter the party with this: "Hello, everyone! Thank you for coming, and I can't wait to spend the next 45 minutes or less with you tonight." This sets the expectation. Then, true to your word, and 45 minutes later, raise your glass and say, "Thank you all for coming. Get out."

When someone invites you to something you don't want to go to, say, "Oh, my gosh! Thank you for asking. This sounds amazing, and I'd love to go, but I just don't want to. Thank you!" This actually works, and your decline doesn't register with the person inviting you until about four minutes after you've walked away.

If you see someone in a god-awful show and they were terrible in it, never be rude. Mike took this very personally. He knew he was terrible in some terrible shows over the years. You could say, "I can't believe what you did up there," but that's just bitchy.

When someone has on a new shirt or dress that's pretty but ill-fitted, say, "I love your shirt/dress! Love it! It's just beautiful. Didn't they have it in your size? It's gorgeous." That's a fun one to use.

And to go full circle, get into bed at night, and pray for the world and that you can be the best person you can possibly be all the time...negating a few of Mike's rules.

CHAPTER 38

I was thinking about what Mike used to call "the Abbott and Costello night." This is a great example of the nuances of Cantonese that Mike could never really understand. Yes, it made for comedy, but it really shows how, even after five years of living with Chinese colleagues, an American, specifically Mike, can still not be taught nuance.

There was a new installation on a very famous castle in a Famous Theme Park with a new holiday light spectacular. Mike was standing with his production manager. This is an almost literal conversation with the production manager, Tan.

Tan began, "Ah, Mike. Him wants to see you."

Mike said, "Who?"

"No. Him."

"Who?"

"Him."

Mike was confused, and Tan was very confused.

Mike said, "Who's him?"

"No. Who is who, and Him is him."

Mike points to a worker.

"This one?"

"No. That is Whan. That Wat."

"What?"

"Yes."

"Okay. So, Him wants to speak to me?"

Tan was over it but, trying to be respectful to Mike, said, "No. Him wants to speak to you, not Mee."

"What does he want?"

"Hee does want anything. Him wants to talk with you."

Mike, being very careful now, thought that he had figured out he was being totally dense. He took a deep breath and said, "Okay, Tan. Bring Him over, and he can ask me a question."

Tan said, "Why would Him ask Mee a question?"

"Okay—just bring Him over to me."

"Him does not want to talk to Mee. Should I just bring Him to you?"

"Yes! Tan, please do that!"

Tan, feeling relieved, said, "Okay!"

Mike and Tan shook hands like they had just signed a pact for world peace as Tan went to get Him. Then it hit Mike. Mike's longtime colleague named Him. Him! Of course! They had just had lunch together yesterday. Him! Mike felt stupid; probably because he was stupid. Again, these nuances fell on Mike's deaf ears, and it is also a display of how gracious Mike's Chinese colleagues could be.

And it was these kinds of daily conversations that began Mike's Xanax addiction.

CHAPTER 39

I have not been totally honest. During this time of reflection, as Mike lies there in bed, I'm taken back to when there was a weeks-long loophole. A few weeks when I knew I was distinct from Mike. This was not supposed to happen. The Souls are taught, again not by words, but in the sense of knowing, that a Soul would choose the person and never know that fact until the very end...until now.

But there was a time—a time when the cord tugged enough for me to know.

Mike was suffering terribly in ninth grade, the first year of high school. 1975. Mike was so ill, mentally, and he began to abuse his body. He stopped nourishing himself. Mike could only see a grotesque person, heavy, not worthy of anything. Mike was 75 pounds and had lost touch with reality.

This is now commonly known as anorexia and was largely due to non-acceptance because of his sexuality, which of course, Mike did not know at that time. He just stopped eating one day. He began rituals to punch himself in the stomach 100 times to beat off the fat. He would only eat the outside of food, making sure to leave most of the food behind.

Teachers began to notice. Neighbors did, too. Mike was sure his family, all living together, didn't notice, but they did, and they tried to hide their concern. It was 1975, and this was not a common thing for medical personnel to know anything about. And there was a further complication. As you know, Mike had a risky birth. Albeit a successful birth, Mike had a severe and chronic blood disease called Thalassemia.

This is a blood mutation that makes the person extremely anemic, tired, listless, and prone to dizziness. It also meant Mike's blood cells were also not round. They were concave, both red and white cells, and the cell walls would break down easily. Since Mike was born with this disease, Mike didn't know any different; and yes, he was tired, but he was always tired, and so Mike didn't/doesn't know what it feels like to feel rested.

With all this, there was the self-deprivation of food making the whole mess worse. And this is when I stepped out of Mike. For the first time, I saw Mike, and I was devastated by the amazingly thin boy in front of me. I just had to do something. I was allowed to step out to fix this situation because it was Angel #4's doing. I couldn't have done this on my own. I stepped in and planted the thought in Mike's head that he had to eat. And Mike did eat. He just started to eat. And the immediate problem seemed to fade away.

Mike now realized he had made his life and others' lives a nightmare. Everyone was worried about his health, and yet Mike was more embarrassed than anything else. He went into Maria's family photograph drawer and picked out a whole year's worth of photos of him looking like walking death. Mike felt compelled to destroy the pictures manically. This, of course, was a replacement for other obsessive behavior. But, when you think about it, manic photo ripping as a means of wiping that devastating stage from history was a small price to pay because Mike was finally eating.

I believe this could be the only time that the Source called an Angel to intercede, and that interception was to let me, Mike's Soul, fix the situation. As soon as I stepped back into Mike, I, of course, forgot all about this, and it was only now in this time of reflection that I could recall this Angel's gift to help save Mike's life. And this was a time when a Soul would cry. And I did.

Chapter 40

Bec

Here I am, enjoying all these great memories, and I have no idea if Mike can remember it all, too. I hope he can. We had a fantastic life together. Not all chuckles and grins, but a lot of fun times, for sure. I wondered if he could see himself here in this bed...waiting to die. One thing I know for sure is that if Mike saw those red roses the hospice nurse put on his bedside table, he'd start blabbering on about *Ice Castles* and those "damn roses" and that blind skater.

So many of Mike's "passed" friends and relatives have visited during this last hour. I could see them all, but I don't think they can see me. They look like they're having actual conversations with Mike, but who knows...? The talks could be one-sided.

Mike

What's that smell? Is that...? I smell roses...akk...roses. Those damn roses! Why did they have to throw roses at that poor blind skater? She couldn't see! Such a great film, even though Robby Benson seemed to mumble-lisp through the whole film. Was Leif Garrett busy, and they couldn't get him? I still smell roses.

Oh, here comes Gramma Rose. She was my favorite.

"Gram, why did you leave me your mink stole when you died?"

Rose says, "You always liked to rub your face on it."

"Oh...I did. I always wondered why Gloria didn't get the mink stole."

"Mikey, Gloria was so bad as Alice in *Alice in Wonderland*, why would I leave her a mink stole? And you wore it so well while you pretended to be the Flying Nun in the living room. We will see you soon. Oh, and hi, Charlie."

And she is gone.

Here comes Aunt Connie.

Aunt Connie says, "You were my favorite, even over my own boys."

"I know."

"I know you know." And then Aunt Connie slaps me very lightly like she used to do before she kisses me. "We will see you very soon, Mikey."

"Aunt Connie? Will it be okay?"

"Oh, yeah. It's fine. I mean, it's not Caesar's Palace, but it ain't Circus Circus neither."

Hmm...I thought Heaven would be more than a Las Vegas analogy, but with all the morphine, I'm not so sure these conversations are actually happening anyway.

Aunt Connie drifts out, and another being drifts in.

"Hello, Mike."

"Hello, Brian. How great to see you. You look like an angel."

"I'm not an angel."

"I'm glad you are here. Why are you here?"

"I have to tell you something."

"What is it, Brian?"

"You were the only one I ever loved fully, even after our mutual break up. I just couldn't keep up with you enough to marry you. You were too much, too often."

"I'm sorry, Brian."

"I know. Oh, and Donna and Sheri say hello. I have to go."

"Why? What's so pressing you have to go?"

"Nothing, Mike. It's just what people say when it's time to go. Oh, and by the way, nice hospital gown. Didn't they have it in your size?"

Brian smiles and is gone.

Another figure is entering the room. But I don't recognize the visage.

"I'm Mike."

The figure said, "Now, that can't be right."

Bec

"Oh, this can't be right." I recognize that stupid voice right away.

Really? Not that stupid William Stuckard. How did he get here, and why?

Mike

"No, really. I'm Mike Pennello. Who are you?"

"I'm William Stuckard."

"Do I know you?"

"I don't know. I don't think so. What year is it? Are you dead?"

Bec

What an idiot. He knows how this works. Mike clearly is not dead yet. Stupid.

Mike

"No, I'm not dead. Pretty nearly dead. I've had several visitors in a row, though."

"Anyone I know?"

"How would I possibly know that? What year did you die?"

"1745."

"Okay, it's 2050. So, I'm pretty sure we never met."

"That can't be right. We won!"

"What?"

"The Jacobites defeated the British government forces."

"Oh... That's cool. And really old news. Is that how you died? In the war?"

"Oh, heavens, no. I was at the first Women's Cricket Match in Surrey, England."

"Is that how you died? From the boredom of the cricket match?"

"This can't be right. I can't be here unless I was somehow brought up during the reflection."

Bec

Crap, it was me. Thinking about that idiot brought him here to visit Mike. What an idiot.

Mike

"Well, off I go, what is it, Michael Pennello? Is there a door, good sir?"

"Do you need a door? Everyone one else just drifted."

"Daft, you're right."

Mike & Bec

This man is an idiot.

Mike

William Stuckard leaves the room in a bumbling kind of way. In the bumbling way someone would knock over a lamp or something while trying to leave...if they weren't a vapor-people dead person.

The idiot is replaced by the unmistakable scent of a horrendous cigar. Grampa Jim enters.

"Gramps! You still smell like cigars."

"When something works, Mikey, you just go with it."

"Hey, look who joined you! Grams! Hiya, Grams!"

Cecilia says, "My little Mikey. It's so good to see you. Sing me the alphabet."

"Grams, I have a tube down my throat, and I'm unconscious."

"So that's a no, then?"

"It's a no."

"Mikey, we've watched you your whole life, and we are all so proud of you. Not so much in Hedda Gabler, but all the other stuff. Can't wait to see you on the other side."

Mom comes into the room as Rose, Frank, both grandfathers, Cecilia, and Aunt Connie drift out.

"Mom!"

"Mikey."

"Where's Dad? "

"He's in the same place he was when you were born."

And we said it together: "In the hall."

"Mom, what's it like out there?

"The hall...well, it's mint green..."

"Not the hall, Ma."

"Oh. Well, Mikey, it's not like they told us at church. It's better. It's more equal. Does that make sense? Anything you didn't like or anything you loved or didn't have or had doesn't matter at all. Everyone is equal, and there's a calm sameness."

"Thanks, Ma."

"See you in a bit.

"Ma, one last question. Why didn't anyone ever love me enough to marry me?"

"Mikey, everyone loved you too much to marry you."

Mom leaves the room.

CHAPTER 41

As his loved ones are visiting Mike, I'm in my own world of remembering, thinking about how similar Mike and I are in that we both loved our work. We love collaborating with all the giant minds at Famous Theme Park. We love the seemingly "impossible" becoming a successful event and the teamwork that felt like a real team—the laughs. There was so much laughter through work. Even the time Mikey and the team had to produce the oddly titled shows like *Mouses' Jumpin' Jam* in India.

This show toured throughout Asia, and after each show, the set was scrapped. It was much easier and cheaper to scrap a set and build a new one in the next town than to travel it across Asia by air and freight with a set. When the show was over, the crew went to take down the set and found that two families had moved inside and underneath, making it their home. Funny...sad...odd...and wonderful all at the same time.

India. Throngs of people showed up for this week-long free show. It was amazing how the Famous Theme Park brand resonated so well with all kinds of people all over the world. Those families are long gone, but for that time, that very poor Indian family in Bangalore could say they lived under a very colorful and whimsical set for two famous mice, their two squirrel-like pals, a dog-man in a green hat, a duck and his girlfriend, and a regular yellow dog. Now, this was no *Lifestyles of the Rich and Famous*, but it was no *Love It or List It* either.

Whilst working in India, Mike had a number of strange experiences.

Mike was always fascinated by religions. Perhaps you may remember that he was a Religious Studies major along with a few other majors at Manhattan College. While in India, Mike made a point to go to as many religious celebrations as possible to learn about the culture. India, which is an amazing meld of religion, politics, culture, and social outings, has a holiday almost every day.

But there was one ceremony in particular that Mike just had to check out: It was a celebration of the cow's penis. Yes, you read that correctly. I'm sure everyone knows that, in India, a cow is considered sacred. I'm not so sure that here in the United States that everyone's convinced that a female cow has a penis. However, religion is filled with phallicies...see what I did there...? Even a Soul can be funny, but only once a year. And there's usually ice cream served.

Anyway, it was the festival of the cow's penis. Mike went to the Temple, and surprisingly, it was extraordinarily crowded. There are a lot of rules for these very intense religious events. Arms must be covered; heads must be covered, no shorts, no shoes allowed in Temple, and numerous people sit on mats.

All are usually welcomed, and no one is discouraged from participating in this ritual. There is a ceremony done in Hindi, of course, and Mike understood much of it because it was similar to a Catholic Mass in Latin in that he sort of picked up on the motions and phrases to understand that they were there today to worship the cow penis.

Just to be clear, this is not a transgender cow. It's just a cow. I think it may have been a Dairy Longhorn. (A great drag name, by the way.) Once the ceremony is over, everyone is invited to go in and look into this golden box to see the cow with the penis.

Of course, Mike went up to the box and looked at the sculpted cow with the penis. Well, Mike being Mike, he couldn't let anything go, so he did have to speak to one of the monks on the way out. The conversation went a little something like this.

"Hello. I am Mike from the United States, and I have a question about your religious ceremony that I just saw. Oh, by the way, it was really beautiful, and I love seeing other cultures and their celebrations."

"Thank you for coming, and I know what you're going to ask me."

"Yeah, that penis thing."

The monk looked confused.

"Oh. Forgive me. I guess I didn't know what you were going to ask me."

Mike continued, "What on Earth did you think I was gonna ask you?"

"I thought you were going to ask how to make a donation or make a fruit offering to our altar."

"I can do that. How can I make an offering to your altar...? And what's up with the penis thing?"

"You can make an offering of fruits or vegetables or any food type that we will donate to many families in need around town. Also, the fruits and vegetables that you leave may be consumed by Ganesh."

Mike wanted to say so much more about how it is unlikely a statue will consume food, but he knew he had to control his ability to be irritating. And he really did want to know more about this religion and not to disrespect the monk.

Mike continued, "Okay. So we have a cow here. And I don't know about here, but cows in the United States tend to be female because...well...they're cows. So, I'm just interested how in India, a cow, who also seems female because they give milk and bear children, may also have a penis. And why do you worship this? It seems a little irrational."

"Mike...is that correct? Yes, I believe you said your name was Mike. I understand how you might be confused by this. I think what you're missing is that religion is not rational. If I were to tell you a story about a young girl who becomes pregnant by some means other than actual sex, that a man with wings flies in her window and tells her that something great is going to happen, but he can't tell her what that great thing is, that this other man then dies, and three days later, he rises from the dead, and then you believe that one God person is actually three God persons, the Father, the Son, and the Holy Spirit, and that a simple wafer and glass of wine is transformed into the actual body and blood—which is cannibalism by the way—of Jesus Christ is perfectly logical, does a cow with a penis seem all that strange?"

Ouch.

Mike cleared his throat. It went so dry.

Mike managed to get out, "That altar again, for the fruit, it's where again?"

"Over there. And don't forget your shoes on the way out."

CHAPTER 42

As my mind wandered to my top three favorite memories together, it felt like Mike might be remembering them, too. The feeling was slight, but it felt like a lighter version of when we were together. The possibility of Mike and I remembering in tandem was kinda cool.

Mike did some pretty amazing projects in his lifetime, but creating a show for the United States White House for an event developed by one of the world's most sophisticated and brilliant minds, Michelle Obama, had to be one of the top three events and one of my top three memories. Mike and the fantastic Famous Theme Park Team put on a show in the West Ballroom. It was the story of *The Jungle Book*. A story about coming together, friendship, and diversity. This was a milestone for not only for Mike, but the entire company he worked for. That is the first time the company had ever been invited to perform at the White House, so it had to go perfectly.

And perfect it was...but there is so much more to it that makes it a perfect "Mike" story.

The performance was for Michelle Obama's state luncheon. It was the last state luncheon and served as the final formal function of the Obama administration. The State Luncheon was all about First Lady Michelle Obama's efforts to help raise children with a habit of healthful eating along with her "Get Moving" platform as well as the Obama administration's inclusion platform. The show was about love, acceptance, and inclusion.

Mike had rehearsed the intricate, elegant, funny, and expressive storytelling version of *The Jungle Book*, written by Rudyard Kipling and reimagined by Large Theme Park Company. He and his amazing team, most notably a fantastic choreographer named Cindy, staged this show to play in the West Ballroom, including the attending children and esteemed guests, as the State Luncheon's finale. The goal was to create an immersive experience for children to learn about what it takes for an entire group of people, not just one person, to make a real difference in the world. This was a gorgeous show, filled with diversity, not only in the performing cast but with the musicians and staff. The show was well-rehearsed in Central Florida before arriving at the White House.

Mike walked into the West Ballroom, and he and Cindy instantly realized that the show that they staged in Florida would not fit on the stage that was built in the West Ballroom. The dimensions the White House sent to the Large Theme Park Company were far different from those he saw in front of him. Mike had one hour to fix this show before guests were to arrive at the White House.

This is where Mike was at his best. He immediately slipped into his most professional "commander and general" mode with a no-nonsense policy for anyone. Mike walked over to the White House event chief of staff and said, "I need your help to remove everybody except Cindy and the cast of performers. We have a lot of work to do, and we have to move fast."

The event chief of staff said, "I like the way you work, sir. Clearly in charge. Point out to me who needs to leave."

Mike pointed to all non-essential personnel, and those people were immediately escorted out of the room. Mike loved being in charge. He and Cindy began to move like a combination of a cheetah and a weasel around the room as they re-staged the entire show. This was one of the most important events the Large Theme Park Company was ever to do, and Mike and Cindy luckily had the support and faith of their leaders. After all, this was for the country. Also, it was for Mike's most favorite president ever and the first lady. Mike always believed the Obamas were some of the most influential people in the United States' history.

One would think things were going smoothly were they to watch Mike make split-second changes that produced results that looked like they took months of planning. And things were going smoothly...on the outside. Unfortunately, Mike also had to go to the restroom...badly. But he did not have time to go to the restroom. Mike had needed to go to the restroom for hours, but there was much too much work to be done, so he kept plodding onward. And to compound things, Mike did not have the luxury of "going to the bathroom" on the morning of going to the White House because he was just too nervous to go. But now, Mike had to go...like really go.

In other words, Mike was holding back a "stress crap" mother-load...literally. And less literally, a Hoover Dam's worth of the unfortunate double portion of spicy chicken wings and chopped salad he had eaten the night before.

Two firsts were about to happen at the White House that day: The legacy of the musical *The Jungle Book* and the legacy of Mike forever changing the Mamie Eisenhower Memorial bathroom.

There was White House security everywhere. In fact, everyone in the room was attached to a security guard. This was not only for the safety of the performers and the team, but it was the White House, and it had to be secure. The cast was in their dressing rooms, and everything was ready to go. Mike's newly re-blocked show was fully rehearsed, and the show was to premiere in about a half-hour. Mike thought that was the perfect time for him to finally use the restroom. He walked out of the dressing room and started to walk down the hall.

"Excuse me, sir, where are you going?"

Mike turned around and saw an amazingly handsome, blonde, blue-eyed security officer. It was almost like looking at the most beautiful man in the world in a uniform in the White House...well, because he actually was looking at the most beautiful man in the world...in a uniform...in the White House.

"I'm going to use the restroom."

The security guard said, "Yes, sir. The restrooms have been closed and the area secured."

"I don't think you understand that I *reeeeeaallllly* have to use the restroom."

The way Mike said "really" felt like it took a whole minute for him to get out.

"I do understand completely that you do need to use the restroom, sir. And I will take you to the restroom."

Mike told the security guard that he really didn't need to take him to the restroom. He knew how to do that all by himself. But the security guard explained that taking him to the restroom was a necessity to ensure that the White House and its guests remain secure.

"So, sir, please follow me, and we will use the Mamie Eisenhower Memorial restroom."

Mike had so many things spin in his head in one second:

The first thing was that he would channel Tennessee Williams and become Blanche Dubois and say something in a Southern accent like, "Well, thank you, gentleman caller, for accompanying me to the restroom."

The second one was, "Why is there a Mamie Eisenhower Memorial restroom?"

And the third one was he had never been escorted to the restroom by a man in a uniform.

That last sentence might be a lie.

The security guard continued down the hallway.

"Please, follow me, sir."

Mike did as he was told and followed the security officer to the restroom. The security officer opened the door to the restroom, and Mike had a surprise. It wasn't a public bathroom as he had expected. The bathroom was a single person restroom. I guess they literally meant it. It was Mamie Eisenhower's personal restroom.

The bathroom was lovely, simply lovely. There was a lovely toilet and a beautiful double sink vanity, a lovely window with her signature pink draperies, and wallpaper everywhere. Even the commode was pink. The double sinks were pink. The whole damn bathroom was pink...and lovely.

Now, this part is important. There was no wall divider in the room, just a one-person restroom. The security officer closed the door behind them both. Mike suddenly felt like they were two best gal pals who decided to go into the bathroom together, so they could keep the conversation going.

Mike stared at the security officer, and the security officer stared back. Mike finally said something like, "Thank you for taking me to the restroom...I really appreciate it...I feel very safe..."

In other words, Mike did a lot of yammering, thinking that would cause the security guard to leave eventually.

The security guard had to cut Mike off.

"I have to stay with you, sir."

Mike said, "What?"

The security guard repeated, "I have to stay with you, sir. That is the protocol. I escorted you into the restroom, and I must escort you out of the restroom and prove that nothing happened in this restroom that was unusual."

Mike thought, *This whole thing is unusual.*

The security guard turned his back to Mike and faced the pink double sinks, looking away from the commode.

Mike said, "So...um...you expect me...to be able to use the restroom with you standing in here? I mean, right here with me? Do you realize that I've had to go to the bathroom for at least the last six hours? I've *reallllly* had to go, and I fear this will be a memorable dump. Like, not just haha, I'll laugh about it later, memorable... I'm talking maybe it will get its own restroom named after it, memorable! What I do know is that it will not be a good experience for either of us. This toilet will be taught a lesson. I'm even too embarrassed to undress, and at the same time, I really wanna undress because you're really hot." Mike regretted that last sentence.

The security guard said, "Trust me, sir, I've seen it all. You're not the first person I've had to escort to this restroom. I would ask you to just be comfortable, do your thing, and pretend I'm not here. This is fine, sir."

Pretend you're not here! Ha! Sure.

Pretend this gorgeous man in a uniform with gorgeous blue eyes standing in front of the sink with his bubble-butt ass toward Mike in a secret restroom was not here... That would be hard to pretend was not happening considering it was one of Mike's all-time wet dreams and his favorite fantasy.

Well, the fantasy bubble got burst, as the beavers were poking, and it was almost impossible for Mike to hold back the dam any longer.

So, Mike said, "Okay, but I think this is going to be life-changing for both of us."

The security guard did not say a peep. He didn't even move.

Mike tentatively took down his pants and then his underwear. He raised the lid of the toilet, and he gingerly sat down on the pink commode as the wrath of hell was soon to shoot out of his ass. It was something that would make Mamie Geneva Eisenhower, the First Lady of the United States from 1953 to 1961, not only blush but turn over in her grave three times. Mike knew these facts about Mamie, including her middle name, because there was a giant portrait of her in her signature pink gown on the opposite wall of the commode with that information.

And then it began.

Mike began to—how could it be put delicately?—it cannot possibly be put delicately—began to move his bowels for about three minutes straight with an accompaniment of gurgling gas and high-pitched whistles accented by toilet bowl water splashes that would drown out any John Philip Sousa composition. It was endless. Normally, with friends, this endless shit show would be filled with mortified laughter. Not now. Not at the White House. Not in the Mamie Eisenhower Memorial Bathroom. Not behind this Calvin Klein model security guard fantasy.

There was an upside. Mike was grateful that he finally got to go to the bathroom. Mike was embarrassed because of the situation with the security guard, but even more so since Mamie Eisenhower looked like she was judging him from her portrait. As Mike's little crap concert was approaching its end, he wondered how this would all end when they, together, had to walk out of the bathroom.

And then it was done.

Mike was now in a new predicament. There was so much backsplash from this Eisenhower endeavor that there was no way regular toilet paper was going to cut it. Almost panicked, that's when he spied the lovely pink hand towels by the pink double sinks. He took a moment to weigh his options. He could either stand for a picture next to Michelle Obama smelling like a baby's dirty diaper, or he could ask the guard to hand him a moistened pink hand towel. Mike chose the latter, the guard graciously soaked the towel for him and handed it back to Mike without turning around, Mike wiped excessively, tossed the not-so-pretty-anymore pink towel in the trash bin next to the commode, pulled up his underpants and his pants, and put himself back together. He then walked over to the double sink and washed and dried his hands. Mike looked directly at the security guard, and the security guard looked directly at Mike. The only thing Mike could think to say to him was, "Well, that was unexpected."

The two of them left the restroom as if nothing happened. Mike went back to the dressing room, and the show went on perfectly. The security guard went back to his post in a most professional manner. Mike did forever wonder, though, what the security guard said to the other security guards in the break room about the Mamie Eisenhower Memorial Restroom experience.

CHAPTER 43

The second favorite memory is actually more of a trait of Mike's that created some fantastic memories. He had some of the most amazing brushes with celebrities. One time, Mike bumped into Shirley MacLaine on 46th Street, like literally knocking her over and picking her up and then screaming at her, "You're Shirley MacLaine!"

She said, "Yes, that's me. I wonder if you have a minute to hail me a taxi."

"Sure, Shirley!"

Another time, Mike saw Elizabeth Taylor in her stretch limo after a performance of *Little Foxes* on Broadway. Mike pounded on the window and said, "You're Elizabeth Taylor."

She said, "I know," and Mike felt a little ridiculous.

Mike and his long-time friend, Andy, lived on W. 45th St. across from the Martin Beck Theater. On that one stretch of street, they would see Bernadette Peters walking to Sunday in the Park with George at The Schubert, Sigourney Weaver walking to Death and the Maiden, and Liza and Chita walking together into *The Rink* at "The Beck" (Martin Beck Theatre).

During their tenure at the Hildona Court Apartments, they bore witness to many flops as they came in and out of that enormous theater. To name a few flops would be *Big Deal*, *The Rink*, and the quintessentially awful *Bye Bye Birdie*. There were hits there, too. Like *Burn This* with John Malkovich and the long-running *Into the Woods*. That show brings to mind an interesting memory.

Andy and Mike loved hanging out of their window, and Mike had to yell out celebrity names almost every night. It was his odd obsession. He could not stop it. He'd love to tell stars their names. And he didn't want anything else from them. No autograph. Nothing. Just to yell their name. Mike would then feel a bit stupid about it, but he did it anyway.

During the run of *Into the Woods*, Andy and Mike saw that Bernadette Peters would walk down 45th Street on her way to the theater every day. Sometimes they would hear her warming up, but sometimes, she would just be walking. And after many days of window watching, they noticed that it would always be around the same time, usually around 6:45 P.M.

One day, like any other, in their usual perch, Andy and Mike saw her walking past their window, but this day, out of the blue, Andy yelled out, "Hey, Bernadette Peters."

Well, Mike died and fell to the floor.

Miss Peters looked up to the windows and said in her iconic, quietly youthful, on the verge of tears voice, "Hello."

And then she kept walking—like any normal person would do.

Well, Andy and Mike found this fascinating, and the next night, once again Andy yelled out, "Hey Bernie," and Mike added just for fun, "Hello, Miss Peters."

This time she stopped and said, "Hello, boys! What are your names?" They responded with their names, and she responded with, "Well, hello Andy and Mike. It's very nice to meet you. You just hang out of this window all day?"

Mike and Andy said simultaneously, "Yes!"

Then Mike said, "Well, I work...but I am home now...as you can see...I am here."

Miss Peters was very gracious and said, "Well, I look forward to tomorrow's shouting match of hellos."

This went on for a few days.

Mike worked as a concierge at the Milford Plaza Hotel, just one block away, less than a two-minute walk home. The routine went as follows: At shift's end, Mike would come home around 6:30 P.M. He would return to the apartment, catch up with Andy, and then they would go hang out at the window.

But, one day, the routine went a little differently than normal. Mike ended his shift and walked into their second-story apartment, said hi to Andy, and noticed someone was sitting at the table.

It was Bernadette Peters.

So, after a pause and then a rather interesting pacing of words, Mike said, "Well...Hello, Bernadette...Peters. You are Bernadette Peters, and you are here in our living room." Followed quickly by, "Andy, may I see you in the bedroom?"

Andy said, "Yeah...well...sure...okay." Andy then turned to Bernadette Peters. "Bernie, be with you in a minute."

Andy and Mike walked into the bedroom. Mike closed the door for privacy. Their walls were as thin as onion skin paper, so I'm sure Bernadette Peters heard all of this.

Mike said to Andy, "Why is Bernadette Peters in our living room?"

Andy explained she had a sore throat.

"And she is here, why? Are you, all of a sudden, a pharmacist?"

Mike wanted more information why Bernadette Peters appeared to be in their living room.

Andy continued, "Well, I was hanging out the window because I don't work like you because I haven't been able to find a job that I like. You know I've been really looking for a job..."

"Andy, please stay on topic. Bernadette Peters. Living room. Sitting. Why, and please don't say she has a sore throat again."

"Okay, so I'm hanging out the window, and I see Bernie. I say, 'Hey, Bernie! How are you doing today?'

"Bernie tells me her throat is feeling a little sore, and she has to sing a show tonight. I asked her what she does for that. And she said she usually has a hot cup of Throat Coat tea."

Andy pontificated to Mike.

"Mike, Throat Coat is a tea that soothes the vocal cords..."

"Andy, I'm in the theater...I know what Throat Coat is."

"Well, you wanted details."

"I don't need that many details."

"Okay, so do you want me to just skip over to exactly why Bernadette Peters is here?"

"That would be refreshing."

Andy gets all excited and continues. "Okay. So she said she has a sore throat. I say, 'Hey, I have some Throat Coat up here.' I know it's your Throat Coat, but I thought, who cares whose Throat Coat it is because it's Bernadette Peters, and she needs Throat Coat, and you have Throat Coat in the cupboard. So, I thought we'd use that Throat Coat, and I will just tell her it was my Throat Coat."

"Andy, can you please stop saying Throat Coat?"

He said he wasn't sure but continued.

Andy continued, "Bernie thought for a minute down there on the sidewalk, and then she said yeah, she would come up and have tea together. She said we seemed really nice. And she came up, and we've been chatting, and she's lovely, and honestly, she has not cried once."

Mike said, "Why would she cry?"

"It's her thing. You know, I think she's feeling better...and you know what? I think we have saved *Into the Woods* tonight. And now I have to go back to Bernie."

They both left the bedroom and joined Bernadette Peters at the Salvation Army table.

For some reason, Andy was always able to call Ms. Peters "Bernie," but Mike was only able to say her full name every time. He would say things like, "So, Bernadette Peters, where do you live?" And, "Bernadette Peters, how long did it take to rehearse *Into the Woods*?"

And Andy would just blurt out, "Bernie, what's your favorite color of purse?"

And Bernie said, "You know, Andy, I do need a new purse, and I want a pretty green color."

Andy said that he had dated a hot Swede who worked at Bottega Veneta on 5th, and he could get her a "...real bargain. Maybe free if I put out. I mean, a purse is worth it."

And they would just cackle and be all chummy-like.

Mike felt like he was having tea in a horrible two-bedroom apartment in a horrible apartment building with a major star...who needed a purse.

Andy was just having tea with a woman who sings and occasionally gets a sore throat, and who has a bad bag.

And that wasn't the only time Bernadette Peters—alright, Bernie—would show up at the apartment. Over the run of the show, Bernie came over a number of times, either before or after the show, just to chit-chat.

I found her to be an amazing person able to talk about any topic. What I recalled most about Bernie was that she had a passion for many different things; political, social, theatrical, and just the state of the world. And you know something, I think Andy and Mike affected her perspective on things as much as she affected theirs. Bernie could also kill them both at the card game Euchre.

And that is how Bernie or Bernadette Peters and the boys became short-term friends who may have long gone forgotten about each other. Well, let's be honest...the boys never forgot.

Bernadette Peters was not the only famous, talented actor to become friends with the boys because of that window. That window was a magical gateway to great conversations and stories. Quite a few celebrities walked by that window. Here's a very short list: Stockard Channing, Chita Rivera, Liza Minnelli, Jessica Tandy, Rick Moranis, and Joan Collins.

Andy and Mike never really counted Joan Collins. I mean, they themselves had better clothes than Joan Collins, bigger shoulders, and better make up. Now that I'm thinking about it, Andy and Mike's favorite celeb was Stockard Channing. They really loved Stockard Channing. Perhaps it wasn't the worst thing they could do? That was a joke. Sometimes a Soul can make a joke. Sometimes the Soul can land a joke. And as proof above, sometimes a Soul cannot land a joke.

Okay. Same apartment. Same window. Same players. Oh, except this time it wasn't Bernadette Peters; it was Sigourney Weaver...at least to Mike. To Andy, it was always just "Sigourney," but he would always pronounce it, "Sigournayyyy."

As Mike and Andy continued their daily structure of peering out the window and yelling out celebrity's names as they walked by, they saw someone who caught their collective eye. This day, a gorgeous statuesque woman was walking her rather large dog down W. 45th St. on her way to the theater. As she approached the window, Andy said to Mike, "That's Sigourney Weaver."

Mike said, "That's Sigourney Weaver?"

Andy said, "Yes, that's Sigourney Weaver." For some reason, Mike felt compelled to ask again, and Andy said it was, in fact, Sigourney Weaver, "and if you keep asking me, it'll still be Sigourney Weaver."

So, Sigourney Weaver walks by, and Andy yelled out loudly, "Sigournayyyy!!"

She stopped, looked up, and said hello. And then she just stood there. Staring up at them...as if the sun were in her eyes, but it couldn't be because she was completely in the shadow of the building. Mike was the quick thinker here. He said, "I really like your big dog." While Mike was the quick thinker here, he did not, as it happened, come up with the most brilliant thought processes to share with this major star.

Sigourney said, "Well, thank you; it's an English mastiff."

Mike said, "Are there other mastiffs from other countries?"

Sigourney said no and explained that the breed was an English mastiff.

Mike said, "Well, I thought that if there was an English mastiff, that might imply that there might be other kinds of mastiff, so that's why— "

Andy quickly cut Mike off, saying, "Well, it's a lovely English mastiff." Then he glared at Mike next to him and said, "What is wrong with you?" He turned back to Sigourney and said, "It's a lovely dog, and it's also very lovely to see you, Sigourney."

Mike asked where she was off to.

Sigourney Weaver said that she was doing a new play that had just opened across the street at the small theater next to the Martin Beck Theater. It was their opening week in play previews, and she wasn't feeling very good about it. She explained it was a play about holding someone hostage and being tied to a chair.

Andy said, "I call that Saturday night."

Sigourney Weaver found this exceptionally funny. The play she was in was called *Death and the Maiden*. It didn't play a very long time in New York, but it did become a very successful film for her.

Andy told Sigourney that if she ever needed a dog sitter while she was doing the play, she could bring it up to the apartment, and they would take very good care of her English mastiff. Andy glared at Mike and made sure he said it again...English mastiff.

Mike asked what the dog's name was.

Sigourney Weaver said the dog's name was Elizabeth.

Andy asked if that was Elizabeth with a Z or Elizabeth with an S. Sigourney said she had never really thought about it that far, but she guessed she would prefer a Z because she was an English mastiff. Mike felt Sigourney glare at him when she said "English mastiff," seeming to take it quite personally. Mike decided not to say anything else.

Andy said that he and Mike lived in Apt. #202, the second floor of the apartment building, and feel free to drop off Elizabeth at any time. They would be happy to take care of her if she was busy with being held captive and the chair and all.

Mike and Andy thought that it was a really good chat with Sigourney Weaver and also thought that nothing would come of it. They were wrong.

About a week later, there was a knock at the door. Mike answered the door, and standing in front of him was, you guessed it...Sigourney Weaver along with Elizabeth with a Z. Mike, of course, said, "Hello, Sigourney Weaver."

Hearing this through the onion paper-thin walls, Andy rushed out of his bedroom and said, "Sigournaay! And Elizabeth! How nice to see you! What can we do for you today?"

Sigourney explained that she had a long tech rehearsal, a re-write, and a very long day ahead and asked if they wouldn't mind taking care of Elizabeth.

Mike said of course they would take care of Elizabeth. He continued, "We don't have any plans at all. In fact, we were just going to lean out the window waiting for you to walk by just to yell your name. So, it's quite nice that you showed up here on your own and surprised us!" Mike and especially Andy were surprised that Mike didn't crash and burn during his monologue to a celebrity holding a giant leashed mastiff.

Of course, Sigourney had all the food supplies and water dishes for Elizabeth and explained how Elizabeth's "course of day" should go. Sigourney was amazingly gracious and asked if they were being put out too much. Andy said he would rather be put out by Sigourney Weaver than anyone else. Again, Sigourney found this funny. She said, "You know, you boys are funny. Do you know that? You're funny. Also, you're instantly likeably, trustworthy. I don't know why I feel this way, but I do."

Andy and Mike explained that they were very flattered by what she said and that they would take very good care of Elizabeth. Sigourney Weaver said she would be back sometime between 11:00 P.M. and midnight, and she thanked them again.

Andy and Mike found Elizabeth to be difficult. I mean, she was a giant English mastiff. Do you know how often a giant English mastiff has to go to the restroom? Let's just say it seemed like every half hour. Do you know how much a giant English mastiff eats? What a giant Mastiff eats is...well, everything that Sigourney brought to the door. The good part was that the only time Elizabeth barked was when the hooker next door was having sex and was doing her usual fake moaning. Her name was Yolanda. Yolanda was a very good friend of Andy and Mike's.

Of course, she was a sex worker, and sometimes they babysat her daughter while she had a John in her room, but she was the worst at faking having an orgasm. Her fake moans with her English/Spanish combination made her say things out loud like, "Oh, Jesus, you person. Give me that pepper sauce. Make me cough up, you yank." It was very difficult for Andy and Mike to sit through this while playing Chutes and Ladders with Yolanda's daughter, Sarah. Anyway, Elizabeth didn't like it either and barked through most of the sexual experiences. Andy and Mike were thankful for that.

Well, it got to be 11:30 at night, and there was a knock at the door, and there she was, Sigourney Weaver. She had in her hands a welcomed sight. Two bags chock-full of Chinese takeout! Sigourney said that she thought they might be hungry, and it would be really nice to have a meal together for all they did for Elizabeth. Mike could hear Andy thinking, *It would've been really nice to have a couple hundred dollars to take care of your giant mastiff, but I guess a little vegetable lo mein and a steamed dumpling won't kill me.*

They pulled out the table and set three chairs around it, and the three of them ate Chinese food, and the boys got the whole lowdown on the play, what was wrong with it, and how Sigourney Weaver had an idea of how to fix it. It was a time in New York when plays would come and go so fast. It was the eighties, and many of those years were considered to be the "death years" of the theater. There were so many bad shows. Andy and Mike found this interesting because Sigourney Weaver was actually talking to them just as regular people eating Chinese food, talking about what was bothering them. Then Sigourney Weaver asked what Mike and Andy did all day.

Mike said, "Well, mostly, we walked Elizabeth. That dog can poop. I mean, like bowling balls." Suddenly the sweet-and-sour pork just became a little sourer. This made Sigourney laugh hard and then, unexpectedly for an Academy Award nominee, snort. The snort made her laugh even harder. The three of them found themselves around a lousy, cheap kitchen table laughing hysterically, while Elizabeth was finding a corner in that roach-infested apartment to pee a little bit. All of this was underscored by the subtle sounds of Yolanda next door saying, "Yes, Papi...yes, Papi...oh, the crescent roll is so hot-hot, and the oven is ready to burn it, and the butter you give."

Classy.

CHAPTER 44

My absolute favorite memory with Mike doesn't involve a prominent personality, celebrity or high production value event, or anything like that.

It was scuba diving in Hawaii, alone in the vast deep with not one living thing around. The quiet. The empty sea. The sunlight gleaming through, but no fish or sea turtles that usually congregated for bits of lettuce a scuba diver usually brings. Nothingness. The still calm of the weightless vastness. This was the only time Mike's mind went to euphoria.

I revel in that thought for an undetermined length of time.

This moment is interrupted by a nurse who checks Mike's vitals.

The nurse? Well, he looks more than concerned, and my cord pulls—hard.

It's time.

It is indeed time, and then a marvelous thing happens.

The room gets a bit cold, and a vapor forms and begins to twirl ever so delicately in the room, like a sheer cloth dancing gently in a mild wind. The vapor begins to form into a beautiful child, not fully defined, fuzzy all around, and translucent. The child is magnificent and yet accessible. Mike says, "It's Charlie. I can see Charlie!"

It's Charlie.

I can see Charlie!

"You're Charlie."

"Yes."

"Hi, Charlie."

"Hi, Mikey."

"How do you know me?"

"I've always known you."

"I don't understand."

"Do you need to?"

"Yeah...I think so. I'm very inquisitive, you know."

"Oh, I know, Mikey."

"Who are you?"

"Charlie...your uncle. I died..."

"From tuberculosis. Gramma told me. Why did you die so young?"

"So many did, Mikey."

"Why are you with me?"

"The Source."

"The what?"

"You'll see soon."

"Well, I have to ask you. What the hell have you been doing for 89 years?"

"Has it been that long?"

"Yes. I mean, I was bored with a lot of my life. I can't imagine how boring it was to watch me be bored."

"I don't know this word, 'boring.'"

"When nothing happens."

"Nothing never happens."

"Well, what about when I'm sleeping? "

"I'm away."

"Where?"

"I don't know. I go to a place that is like what you were thinking about. You know, in the sea."

"And why are you with me, exactly?"

"I was chosen to help you stay safe and guide your decisions."

"But nothing bad ever really happened."

"I am very good at what I do," Charlie smiles.

I smile back.

Then the most marvelous thing I have ever seen happens.

From that child, Charlie emerges a glow that was so bright, but not hurtful to the eyes. Charlie glows and glistens, and the sheerest and most translucent wings now appear from behind Charlie. Charlie's body begins to fade in and out, but his face is always clear and happy.

"You're an angel!"

"I guess I am. I didn't know."

"You didn't know?"

"No, I didn't. But now I know why I was always with you: To become this. And I thank you, Mikey. I love you, Mikey."

And Charlie disappears.

"Now I know how that happens. And that was Angel # 5."

Mike says, "Who said that?"

Shocked, I say, "You heard that?"

Mike says, "Yes, and I see you."

"I see you, too."

The cord pulls very tight.

I can feel Mike is going to pass, and there are mere seconds left.

"I know you."

"I am you."

"My Soul, right?"

"Yes."

"You have been with me all the time?"

"Longer than Charlie. I was with you from birth. We separate on the last day, and my work is to reflect on your life with you...really for you."

Mike says, "It was a fun ride, right?"

"It was."

"I was sad, too. Lonely. Not many saw."

"Mike, I felt everything you felt. I saw everything you saw."

The cord pulls hard.

"Mike, we have seconds left."

Mike says, "I know. I can feel myself being pulled...to another place. Will we see each other again?"

"We will not."

"Did we live a good life?"

"You know the answer."

I fight to stay for just one second more, as I can see Mike is holding on for one more thing to say.

Mike says, "Bec, it's Bec, right?"

"Yes, Mike."

"Come closer."

I make every effort I can to get closer to Mike.

These will be our last words.

Mike says, "Bec..."

"Yes, Mike?

"The remake of *Ice Castles* in 2010 was terrible."

And then it's done.